She shoved him. "If you won't help me, get out of my way!"

In self-defense, Griff reached for her again, pinning her flailing arms to her sides.

"Let go of me!"

"Shh," he whispered. "Shh. We'll find her. We'll save your baby. I swear."

He pulled her closer, his heart pounding at the feel of her supple body in his arms. He was bound by his badge to find her child, and he knew the best way to do that....

"Emily needs me," she whispered against his neck, her breath warm, her tears at first hot, then quickly cooling against his sensitized skin.

Clenching his jaw, he gripped her upper arms and set her away from him.

She eyed him suspiciously. "Are you letting me go?"

He shook his head in defeat. "Sunny, I'll help you... We'll go together."

LULLABIES AND LIES
MALLORY KANE

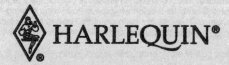

HARLEQUIN®

TORONTO • NEW YORK • LONDON
AMSTERDAM • PARIS • SYDNEY • HAMBURG
STOCKHOLM • ATHENS • TOKYO • MILAN • MADRID
PRAGUE • WARSAW • BUDAPEST • AUCKLAND

For Denise Zaza
With gratitude and respect

ISBN 0-373-88673-X

LULLABIES AND LIES

Copyright © 2006 by Rickey R. Mallory

ABOUT THE AUTHOR

Mallory Kane took early retirement from her position as assistant chief of pharmacy at a large metropolitan medical center to pursue her other loves, writing and art. She has published and won awards for science fiction and fantasy as well as romance. Mallory credits her love of books to her mother, who taught her that books are a precious resource and should be treated with loving respect. Her grandfather and her father were both steeped in the Southern tradition of oral history, and could hold an audience spellbound with their storytelling skills. Mallory aspires to be as good a storyteller as her father. She loves romantic suspense with dangerous heroes and dauntless heroines. She is also fascinated by story ideas that explore the infinite capacity of the brain to adapt and develop higher skills.

Mallory lives in Mississippi with her husband and their cat. She would be delighted to hear from readers. You can write to her c/o Harlequin Books, 233 Broadway, Suite 1001, New York, NY 10279.

Books by Mallory Kane

HARLEQUIN INTRIGUE
620—THE LAWMAN WHO LOVED HER
698—HEIR TO SECRET MEMORIES
738—BODYGUARD/HUSBAND*
789—BULLETPROOF BILLIONAIRE
809—A PROTECTED WITNESS*
863—SEEKING ASYLUM*
899—LULLABIES AND LIES*

*Ultimate Agents

CAST OF CHARACTERS

Sunny Loveless—This lovely private investigator believes in happy endings, until her six-month-old daughter is kidnapped. Now her baby's life hangs on her ability to keep the kidnapper's identity a secret.

Griffin Stone—This FBI agent specializes in missing-child cases. He will die to save Sunny's baby, with or without her help, but in his broken heart he knows there are no happy endings.

Janie Gross—This plain Jane successfully operated a baby-selling ring for years, until Sunny started digging into her past.

Bess Raymond—Jane's old nanny has a secret, one she'd give her life to protect. Will she sacrifice Sunny's baby rather than lose her own daughter?

Hiram Cogburn—The down-on-his-luck ambulance chaser didn't know what he was getting into when he agreed to help his former college buddy deflect Sunny's investigation.

Burt Means—Sunny's testimony put her adopted baby's biological father in prison, and Means is the type to hold a grudge. But how far will he go for revenge?

Prologue

0 hour

Sunny Loveless laughed as Emily reached for the silver rattle. "Not now, sweet Emily Rose," she said. "We'll play Drop the Rattle when we get home. I have to pay the nice lady for the groceries."

Emily gurgled happily.

The grocery clerk grinned. "So you get pureed peaches tonight, Emily? You are growing so much. Sunny, I swear she's bigger every time I see her."

"Six months old last week," Sunny said proudly.

"It doesn't seem that long since you brought her home."

Sunny smiled, remembering the day Emily became her daughter. "I know. She was so tiny. Not even a week old. My lawyer had everything arranged for the adoption by the time she was born." She looked down at her happy baby. "Isn't that right, Emily? Every little thing."

Sunny's heart took flight when Emily smiled and waved her arms. Six months ago, she'd never have believed she could love so much. Her heart felt full to bursting.

"Here you go." The clerk handed Sunny her purchase. "I double bagged it for you. Be careful out there. That rain's really coming down."

"I will. Thank you, Callie."

Sunny rolled the grocery cart to the rear door, slung the bag over her arm and unbuckled the infant safety seat from the grocery cart. Then she fished out her car keys and looked out at the dark wet parking lot. The streetlights were nothing more than pale circles through the downpour.

"Okay, Emily. Let's make a run for it." She took a good grip on the infant seat and smiled at Emily before pulling the hood up to protect her from the rain.

Shouldering the door open, she lowered her head and hurried toward her car, pressing the remote key lock. She threw open the rear door and tossed the grocery bag inside. Then she set Emily's infant seat into the waiting car carrier and buckled the straps.

Water dripped down her daughter's face. She

wiped it away. "Oh Emily, you're soaked. We'll have to take a bath when we get home, won't we?"

Sunny felt the rain intensify, driving through her cotton top and tailored slacks. She shivered. She was soaked, too.

"Good thing it's only a few blocks, right, sweetie?" She straightened and took a step backward to close the car door.

A noise, barely audible over the roar of the rain, reached her ears. Shoes, crunching on gravel.

She started to turn. Suddenly, something came down over her head, blinding her.

She screamed and pushed at it.

A blow to the back of her knees knocked her to the ground. She went down hard, scraping her palms and knees on the asphalt.

"No!" she screamed, and gulped a mouthful of wet, smelly wool. She clawed at it, kicked, tried to fight the thing attacking her.

Something slammed into the small of her back. She lost traction. Her hands and feet scraped along the asphalt as a bony knee forced her flat.

Rough hands jerked the blanket away and grabbed her hair. Sunny couldn't see because of the rain, but she heard Emily cry.

"Stop it! Help!" she cried, but the knee in her

back kept her from taking a whole breath. Brutal hands slammed her head against the asphalt.

Two leather-covered fingers pushed something into her mouth. It tasted like paper.

"Chew on this, Loveless." The voice had substance but no tone. It was a whispered growl.

Her head was slammed into the pavement again, dazing her. Then silence.

Rain splashed in her face. She heard the crunch of gravel again, and a car started and pulled away.

She tried to rise but her hands and feet slipped on the wet asphalt.

"Help!" she cried, knowing her voice was too weak for anyone to hear.

With all her strength, she pushed herself up onto all fours.

"Emily!" She crawled over to the backseat of her car.

"Hey, sweetie. You okay?" She pulled herself to her feet and leaned in to check on her baby.

The infant seat was gone.

Emily was gone.

"Emily?" she called, feeling around on the seat, checking the floorboard. "No! Emily!"

It couldn't be! She had to be here.

Dazed and shivering, Sunny remembered her assailant's words.

Chew on this.

Paper. She clawed the piece of paper out of the

corner of her mouth and spread it open, holding it under the car's dome light.

The paper was wrinkled and wet. She wiped her eyes.

You've messed with the wrong person this time Loveless. Tell the police anything about me and your kid will die.

...your kid will die.

Horror shattered her soul.

"No!" It was a prank. A nightmare. She pushed wet hair out of her face. "Emily!" she screamed, her baby's name ripping from her throat.

A hand gripped her shoulder and she shrieked, but it was the grocery clerk.

"Sunny! I was on my way home. What's wrong?"

"My baby! Someone knocked me down and took Emily!" She sobbed and closed her fist around the note.

The clerk gasped. She pulled out her cell phone. "I'll call the police."

"No! Wait!"

But the woman was already dialing.

You've messed with the wrong person...your kid will die.

What was she going to tell the police?

Chapter One

15 hours missing

"The case is in Nashville?" Special Agent Griffin Stone took the file from his boss and opened it.

Nashville. Just the name of his hometown started a hollow ache in his chest. He'd never intended to go back there.

"I'd rather not—" he started, but Mitch Decker was still talking.

"It's a missing child, a six-month-old infant. The mother was assaulted and the infant grabbed about eight thirty last night outside a grocery store near her home."

The ache in Griff's chest intensified. "Why isn't the local agent handling it? Or CAC?"

"The local agent is a rookie. And the Head of the Crimes Against Children Division asked specifically for you, and I agreed," Decker said quietly, his tone carrying both authority and compassion. "He knows your history with Nashville, and your experience with missing children."

In Griff's mind, those two facts made him unsuitable for the job. "I'd have figured that after the Senator's son—" The bitterness in his voice scraped his throat.

"That wasn't your fault."

Not your fault.

He'd known those words would come back to haunt him someday. He'd been fourteen the first time he'd heard them. He hadn't believed the FBI agent then, and he didn't believe Decker now.

"I was too slow. Waiting for backup was a mistake."

"Waiting for backup was your only option. The kidnappers could have still been in there."

Self-disgust wormed its way through him. "No, it wasn't my only option. If I'd gone on in—if I'd gotten to him five minutes earlier—Senator Chapman's son would be alive."

Decker stood and came around the desk. He placed a hand on Griff's shoulder. "You did everything right. And as always, you went far beyond the call of duty."

Everything right. *Yeah.* Griff was sure that gave a lot of comfort to the Senator when he walked past his son's empty bedroom night after night.

"Look, Griff. I wouldn't send you if I wasn't sure you can handle it."

Decker's belief in him was the only thing that kept Griff from begging him to send someone else.

He cleared his throat. "So what's the interest of the Division of Unsolved Mysteries in this case?"

"A little over a month ago, someone broke into Sunny Loveless's home, sabotaged her computer and took her case files. Since then—"

"Case files?" Griff interrupted. Despite his aversion to anything connected with Nashville, the words piqued his interest. He looked down at a faxed copy of a newspaper article, catching Decker's nod out of the corner of his eye.

"Ms. Loveless is a private investigator."

"Loveless, Inc.," Griff read. "We specialize in—"

Decker's mouth turned up in a wry smile. "Happy endings. I saw that."

No such thing. The response sprang automatically into Griff's head, surprising him. When had he become that cynical? Cynicism implied a loss of hope. The ache in his chest intensified.

Who'd have thought he had any hope left to lose?

"Apparently her specialty is reuniting families, friends who have lost touch, that kind of thing. She's only had her license for two years."

"Two years. Still, she could have racked up a few disgruntled customers."

"Yeah. All the information we have on her previous cases is there." Decker crossed his arms and propped a hip on the corner of his desk. "Anyhow, as I was saying, since the break-in, there have been several seemingly unrelated threats and incidents. There are notations about them in the file."

"Phone calls, vague threats." Griff turned a page. "Some mild vandalism that may or may not be related." He looked up. "Sounds like whoever took her case files has been using the information in the files to harass her—or maybe to blackmail her."

Decker nodded. "Now, her child has been kidnapped. Nashville PD is asking for the FBI's help."

"So they believe the abduction is related to one of Ms. Loveless's cases? What about *her* family? The baby's father?" Griff flipped pages. "Here it is. Ms. Loveless adopted the infant at birth. Biological mother is a teenager." He turned another page, and scanned the information. "Is she married? Divorced? Other children?"

"No. Ms. Loveless has never been married. She was a foundling herself. Adopted by an older couple who have since died. I suspect that explains her *happy endings* business. The baby she adopted is the child of a runaway teen she located—one of her cases."

"Which one?"

"June of last year. Elliott."

"Here it is, Brittany Elliott, a fifteen-year-old, ran away with her twenty-year-old boyfriend. Loveless's testimony put the boyfriend in prison." The missing child's biological father. Definitely a suspect.

"Any contact from the kidnapper? A demand for ransom?"

"Nothing—that we know of."

Griff raised his eyebrows at the tone in his boss's voice.

"The local police lieutenant isn't convinced Ms. Loveless is telling the whole truth."

"He thinks the kidnapper has contacted her." Griff stood, preparing to leave Decker's office. "I shouldn't waste any time. I'll fly out this afternoon."

Decker rounded his desk and sat down as Griff turned toward the door.

"Griff."

He looked back over his shoulder.

"Good luck."

Back at his desk, Griff pulled his laptop toward him and opened his personal database of missing children cases. He'd started it fifteen years ago, using a spiral notebook and a pencil. Now it was computerized in a spreadsheet.

He filled in the fields. Name—Emily Rose Loveless. Age—six months. Date of disappearance—June 20. Location—Nashville, Tennessee.

He stared at the screen for a couple of seconds, then dropped his head between his hands. He wasn't sure he could handle another missing child case.

Ever since that day fifteen years ago when his baby sister had been kidnapped, he'd aimed toward one goal—to save as many children as he could. And, in all honesty, to atone. But few as his failures had been, each one had taken something from him, something the successes never quite replenished. Then, the death of the Senator's son had eaten away too much.

No matter how many children he saved, the hole inside him never got any smaller. Lately, he felt like an empty shell.

Just a few weeks ago, after the Senator's case, he'd talked with Decker about transferring to a specialty that was less emotionally draining, like white-collar crime. With his master's degree in criminal justice, and his eight years' experience, he could work in just about any area.

Now Decker, one of the few people in the world who knew Griff's history, was sending him back to Nashville. To his hometown, where failure and guilt lurked, ready to ambush him at every familiar fork in the road.

The imprint of Decker's hand burned his shoulder, sending a clear message. His boss was depending on him.

Shoving aside his feelings, he booked the next flight out and started preparing himself mentally. This wasn't a personal mission, he reminded himself. It was an assignment.

An important part of his job was to present a calm, comforting exterior to the missing child's frightened mother.

He called the Division's computer expert. "Natasha, hi. Did Decker ask you to run a background check on Sunny Loveless?" He spelled her last name.

"I was just about to call you. I'll e-mail the intel to you so you'll have it on your laptop."

"Good. Thanks."

He saw the icon appear that told him he had new mail. "Okay, got the e-mail. Thanks, Nat."

He hung up, then opened the file labeled LOVELESS and began to read.

But he couldn't banish the question that echoed in his brain and pounded into his chest with each heartbeat.

Why did it have to be Nashville?

18 hours missing

BABY POWDER *and the sour smell of spit-up milk.*
Ugh. Janie Gross nearly gagged as she lit a cigarette and took a deep puff. Her brand new Lexus
stunk of baby. She'd have to get it detailed to get
rid of the disgusting stench.

At least Bess hadn't balked at keeping the kid.

Her old nanny had not been happy about Janie
showing up with another kid, over three years
after they'd agreed to quit the *adoption* business.

Bess was such a sucker for a baby. The brat
would have the best of care. And after fifteen years
of Bess keeping kids while Janie made arrangements for their *adoption,* Janie knew for a fact that
she could trust the old woman.

She grinned at her own brilliance. Handing
over the first kid she'd ever snatched to Bess to
rear as her own was the best investment Janie
had ever made. Lucky for Janie, Bess's own little
boy hadn't been dead six months when Janie had
shown up at her door that long-ago day with a
screaming toddler in tow.

She shuddered. Thank goodness Bess loved
kids, because Janie hated them. Maybe they
should have gone into dog snatching, she thought
with a smile as she merged onto the New Jersey
Turnpike and headed back toward New York.

Dogs were a lot quieter, and a whole lot less trouble.

But nothing she'd ever done in her life gave her the rush she got from snatching a kid from under its mother's nose. And she was good at it. Her nondescript features and colorless appearance made her nearly invisible.

She'd never even come *close* to being caught.

Her cell phone rang. She glanced at the ID, sighed and pressed the speaker phone. "Hi, Eddie."

"Janie, where are you? I thought you'd be back by now." Eddie's voice was tight and high with tension.

"I'm on the road. I'll be home in a couple of hours."

"How was your mom?"

Janie almost laughed. As if she'd ever visit her mother. Eddie was so gullible. He knew how much she hated the woman who had given birth to her but never wanted her, and still he bought her lies about visiting the old hag.

"She's fine. Said to say hi." No way was she telling her husband where she'd really been, or what she'd done. He'd panic again, and screw things up even worse than he already had.

He'd just wanted to help, he'd said.

Janie took a long drag and let smoke drift out

through her nostrils. Eddie's *help* was what had set all this in motion in the first place. If he helped any more, they'd be in jail.

He needed to focus on getting elected. Which reminded her—she glanced at the time. "Shouldn't you be filming those new campaign ads?"

"We're on a break. I'm sick of saying 'I'm Edward A. Gross, and I approved this message.'"

"Well, you just keep saying it, and come November you can say 'I'm *Congressman* Edward A. Gross, from the great state of New York.'"

"Janie? I can't stop thinking about that private investigator and the client she was representing. Maybe we should meet with the girl. Admit she's our biological child. Maybe it could be a positive thing—you know, reaching out to our long-lost daughter—"

"No!" Janie angrily whipped the Lexus into the next lane, and a car swerved, its horn blaring.

Why couldn't Eddie just stick to what he was good at—glad-handing and pandering—and leave the thinking to her? She lowered the window a crack and tossed out the cigarette butt, then lit up another one and took a deep drag while Eddie named all the politicians who had gone on to success after admitting an early indiscretion.

"But Janie, if she *is* one of our babies—"

"Eddie, shut up! You never know who's listening. We don't have any kids. Never change the story, remember?"

She'd drummed the phrase into his head for fifteen long years, ever since the day she'd snatched the first kid. They'd fled Nashville that night, leaving everything behind, including their own two babies whom they'd sold at birth to eager childless couples. It had always been laughably easy to find people willing to pay for a kid.

"But Janie," his voice lowered to a coarse whisper. "The Loveless woman showed me a picture. The girl is eighteen. That's how old our daughter would be. She looks like you."

Janie's ears burned with rage and a dull, throbbing ache started in her temple. "We don't have any children, remember? The story?"

She consciously relaxed her face and throat. She had to calm down. If Eddie thought she was angry at him, he'd fall apart. "Go look nice for the cameras, Mr. Future U.S. Congressman. Concentrate on that bright future. I'll take care of the past."

She flipped off the phone, pounded her palm against the steering wheel and cursed loudly.

Damn that Loveless woman. This was all her fault. A month ago, when Eddie had told her about the private investigator who'd shown up at his office looking for her young client's biological mother, Janie had nearly passed out from shock. Until that moment she'd never spared a thought for the two babies she'd birthed and sold while Eddie was in law school in Nashville. She'd never wanted kids. They were a commodity, nothing more.

The idea that those kids were now teenagers, nearly adults, had never crossed Janie's mind. If the truth about illegally selling their own kids came out, Eddie's future would be down the toilet. They might even go to jail.

Eddie had a real chance to win that House seat. It was what he'd always wanted and whatever Eddie wanted, Janie made happen. She'd worked hard to get them where they were today. Nobody was going to spoil her plans.

The Loveless woman had shown up at the worst possible time.

To give him credit, Eddie had handled her pretty well—for him. He'd lied, told her they didn't have any kids. But Janie knew how bad a liar he was. Then he'd gone and called that dork buddy of his from law school, Hiram Cogburn. Hiram had come in handy to handle any legal matters related to the baby-selling business, but Janie didn't trust him, never had.

Spooked that Loveless had found them so easily, and worried about that fool Hiram's bumbling attempts to throw suspicion elsewhere, Janie had headed for Nashville to assess and contain the damage Hiram had already done.

She'd had no clue what she was going to do about Sunny Loveless, until she'd seen her—with her six-month-old infant.

Even now, the thrill of that moment sent an addictive rush of adrenaline surging through her.

Sunny Loveless had a baby. And babies were Janie's specialty.

34 hours missing

SUNNY LOVELESS paced the length of the interrogation room at the East Nashville Patrol Sector headquarters, her limbs twitching from tension, her head pounding, her empty stomach cramping from the reek of stale cigarette smoke and old coffee.

Nausea burned her throat. Momentarily dizzy, she grabbed the back of a chair and closed her eyes until the wave of sickness passed. It was exhaustion—she knew that. Combined with fear and grief and a terrible, suffocating guilt.

She shouldn't be here, waiting to talk to the FBI agent that Lieutenant Carver had called in. She should be at the operations center the police had set up, reviewing the tips and photos that had come in since the AMBER alert was posted. Or at home, helping Lil recreate the stolen case files that the police had dismissed until two days ago.

She glanced at her watch. They were late.

Not that she was looking forward to going through the events of Tuesday night again, this time for the FBI. Having to remember everything she'd told the police—and everything she hadn't.

She gripped the chair more tightly and shuddered. Not even the FBI could help her. Not with this.

The note that had been stuffed into her mouth by those wet, gloved fingers now rested like a lead weight in the pocket of her slacks. She hadn't let it out of her possession for an instant. It was her only link with her baby.

Her baby. All the horror overwhelmed her again—the attack, the realization that Emily was gone, the sickening sound of that whisper echoing over and over in her ears.

Chew on this, Loveless.

The wooden door creaked open, startling her out of her thoughts. Lieutenant Harry Carver stepped in. "Thanks for coming down here again, Ms. Loveless."

He moved farther into the room and Sunny spotted a taller man behind him.

The FBI agent.

Sunny gave him a quick once-over. He was a

shade under six feet tall, lean and athletic, with dark hair and eyes. He carried himself with a loose-limbed grace that wasn't hidden by the crisp shirt and summer-weight jacket he wore, although his face and the set of his mouth told her he was anything but loose.

His jaw was strong and square. His features were even, but a little too prominent to be considered handsome.

And those eyes were as piercing as an eagle's. She felt an odd mixture of wariness and reassurance. She was going to have to watch her step around him.

"This is Special Agent Griffin Stone. He's with the Division of Unsolved Mysteries."

"Unsolved mysteries?" Fear congealed into a cold knot in her belly. "Is my daughter's abduction connected with an unsolved case?"

"Nothing like that, Ms. Loveless," Agent Stone said, stepping forward.

Sunny noticed his slight accent. He'd grown up in the South.

"I'm here because I've worked a number of missing child cases."

A shadow crossed his face as he spoke. Her investigator's instinct kicked in. He didn't want to be here. Why?

"I see." She held out her hand. "I'm Sunny

Loveless. But then you know that, don't you, Agent Stone?"

Griff lowered his gaze to Sunny Loveless's outstretched hand, and accepted her intense scrutiny. Families of abducted children were initially wary of law enforcement, especially if they'd received a warning from the kidnappers.

For some reason, he was reluctant to touch her. Just seeing her straight slender silhouette, haloed by the faint light from the dingy window, had been enough to slam him in his solar plexus. It was always difficult to meet the family of a missing child for the first time. This time, maybe because he was back in Nashville, the intensity of his reaction surprised him.

But he didn't want to be rude so he took her hand. Her trembling fingers telegraphed how hard she was working to stay in control. After a brief but surprisingly strong grasp, she withdrew.

His hand tingled, as if she'd left a part of herself on him. He knew she'd taken something of him with her. But then each family he worked with took something from him, and gave him something back.

"I'm very sorry about your daughter, Ms. Loveless," he said politely, studying her. She was dressed for business in tailored black pants, high-heeled shoes and a white sleeveless top with a long row of buttons down the front. Her frightening ordeal had certainly left its marks. The palm that had touched his was scraped. Red scratches ran up the left side of her face to her temple, where a bruise wasn't quite covered by her hair. Her eyelids were red-rimmed, and below the angry scratches the creamy perfection of her skin was marred by tear-chapped cheeks. On her left shoulder, a flesh-colored bandage strip peeked out from under the white top.

When he finally met her gaze, he ran smack into green eyes that reflected a dull anguish and a desperate hope he knew all too well.

She immediately turned her attention to the lieutenant. "Do you have any news?" she asked Carver.

"We've talked to several of your former clients. Just like you said, they all seem satisfied with your work."

"What about the break-in, the odd phone calls?"

"Ms. Loveless, I have apologized that the burglary of your case files was not given the attention it should have been back when it happened. But we're on it now, checking alibis in case there's a link between the burglary and your daughter's abduction."

"Any more information from trace evidence?"

Carver shook his head. "CSU didn't find much.

Your clothes had a few dark blue wool fibers. We figure they came from the blanket. Nothing else. The rain pretty much destroyed any evidence at the crime scene."

Pretty much was an understatement. Griff had already gone over the meager evidence with Carver earlier this morning. According to the Crime Scene Unit, the parking lot and Ms. Loveless's car had been washed clean. He'd asked them to go over both one more time.

He cleared his throat. "Why don't we sit down," he suggested, touching the back of a wooden chair in invitation.

When she hesitated, he backed away a step and took a seat himself, then nodded at Lieutenant Carver.

Carver got the message. "I'll be at my desk if you need me for anything." He opened the door and lifted his hand to touch an invisible hat brim. "Ms. Loveless."

She nodded stiffly. "Thank you, Lieutenant."

When the door swung shut behind him, she crossed her arms and looked down at Griff, her emerald eyes bright. "What can you do for me that the police can't, Agent Stone?"

A reluctant admiration eased the knot in Griff's stomach as he leaned back in his chair. Taking a good look at her, he gauged her by the system he'd invented to help him gain the trust of distraught parents.

She was doing her best to appear tough, in control. That didn't surprise him.

Since she was a private investigator of sorts, he'd expected her to be demanding—wanting more effort, minute-by-minute reports, faster results. But he didn't want to be too quick to judge by outward appearances. They could lead to the wrong conclusion.

Carver had said she was *strung tighter than a well-tuned banjo.* It was a good description. Most people would think, given the circumstances, she was holding up remarkably well.

But Griff already knew it was an act. He recognized the hollow fear that emanated from her like a scent. The fear that she would never see her daughter again.

She was barely holding herself together. His heart squeezed in compassion. He immediately quashed the unwanted emotion and called on the careful balance of distance and concern that worked for him. Becoming too emotionally involved would cloud his thinking.

"I can help you, Ms. Loveless. But to do that, I need to hear your account of what happened."

"You have my account in the police report. There's no need to waste time repeating it."

"I thought you were a private investigator."

"I am." Her delicately arched brows knit together in a tight frown.

"Then you know that having the person go over events several times allows new memories to surface."

"I know that it's a tried-and-true tactic to catch people in a lie."

Griff almost smiled. "Does that bother you?"

"No."

She answered too quickly. Griff glanced at her folded arms. Her knuckles were white where her hands squeezed her upper arms.

Body language always told the truth. Ms. Loveless was definitely hiding something.

He let his mouth stretch in a grim half smile. "Good. That should make it easy then, because I like to ask my own questions, face-to-face."

Sunny bit back the urge to snap at him and pressed her lips together instead. She didn't like Griffin Stone. He was like his name. Cold. Hard. Unyielding.

When their gazes had first collided, she'd noticed a hint of sadness and empathy in his dark eyes, as if he knew her pain. But nothing marred his sculpted features now, except a slight frown and a shrewd curiosity that worried her.

His knowing gaze scrutinized everything about

her, from her stance to the way her folded arms pushed up against her breasts.

Suddenly self-conscious, she tried to relax her arms by her sides, but her hands shook. So she sat and clasped them in her lap.

She dreaded reliving that night of hell. Dreaded having to keep her story straight. *Again.*

"Okay," she sighed. "Ask your questions. But could you please hurry? This is a waste of time you could be using to find my daughter."

Her daughter. The words still thrilled her, even as they tore at her heart. She'd always wanted to adopt a baby, to pay forward the boundless love her adoptive parents had given to her. Emily had changed her life in ways she hadn't even imagined.

Now her baby was in the hands of a stranger. Sunny had promised Emily she'd keep her safe, and she hadn't. Her vision clouded.

"Tell me about the attack. Start when you got to your car."

Sunny closed her burning eyes. "Do we have to do this right now? Emily is out there—"

"Trust me. It's not a waste of time."

She heard the sympathy and assurance in his voice, but she also heard a steely determination. Nothing would stop this man.

Certainly not the lies of a terrified mother with secrets to hide.

She blinked and focused on her hands, because she couldn't meet his steady gaze. She was afraid his sharp dark eyes would see past her lies. She couldn't take that chance. He was there to uncover every shred of evidence. She couldn't trust him. She didn't dare.

"It was pouring rain. I threw the groceries into the backseat, then—" She halted as the door to the interrogation room opened.

A young man set two cups on the table, and tossed some packets of sugar and a couple of stirrers down beside them.

"The lieutenant said you might want coffee," he commented over his shoulder as he left.

Griff took one of the cups and pushed the other one toward her.

"Sugar?"

Caught up in the memory of those terrible few minutes when Emily was kidnapped, Sunny shook her head. Her stomach clenched. She wrapped her fingers around the warm cup and stared into the coffee's muddy depths.

"Go on." The agent's soft voice compelled her.

"It was still raining when I got Emily's carrier fastened into the safety seat. We were both soaked. As I straightened, someone threw a blanket over my head and kicked my legs out from under me. I fell on my hands and knees. He pushed me down and slammed my head into the asphalt until I couldn't move."

She turned the cup with shaking fingers, and watched the dark liquid swirl. "As soon as I could pull myself up, I reached into the backseat for Emily—"

She couldn't go on. The horror that had enveloped her soul at the sight of the empty carrier still took her breath away.

"What happened to the blanket?"

"What?" Momentarily startled, she looked up at him. "I guess he took it with him. Maybe he wrapped—" Her breath caught. Had he wrapped Emily in that wet, smelly blanket?

"You didn't see the kidnapper?"

She shook her head. At least that was true. "I should have been faster, stronger."

The agent didn't respond. The fact that he was all business was a relief. She'd had all she could take of trite, well-intentioned but meaningless reassurances.

"Are you sure it was a man?" he asked.

"No. The person was not big. I suppose it could have been a woman. His—" She stopped. She'd almost said *his voice.* She hadn't told anyone that the kidnapper had spoken to her.

As if he'd read her mind, Agent Stone asked, "Did he say anything?"

Sunny swallowed, trying to block out the echo of the ominous whisper in her ears. *Chew on this, Loveless.* She shook her head.

"Okay. What happened next?"

"I crawled around, looking under the car, and— and all around. I thought maybe—" she choked on a wry laugh "—maybe the carrier had slipped off the seat. Maybe Emily had somehow fallen. Maybe..."

Suddenly, vividly, the taste of wet paper and leather flooded her mouth and the memory of kneeling there in the backseat of her car, clawing the note from her cheek, reading its ominous contents, overwhelmed her.

She'd stuffed it into the pocket of her jeans as the grocery clerk rushed up. She couldn't tell anyone about the note. The kidnapper knew her name. He'd threatened to kill Emily.

"Ms. Loveless, I know this is difficult, but I promise you, it will help."

She didn't look at the agent. She had to push the grief back, so she could concentrate on her story.

She patted her cheeks, trying to mask the truth, trying to look innocent under the sharp eyes of the FBI agent, acutely aware of the note burning through her pocket to her skin.

The kidnapper was deviously clever. By not

giving her any hint of who he was, he'd left Sunny with nothing to gain by telling the police about the note—and everything, her child's life—to lose.

Tell the police anything about me—

Who? The question had been screaming through her mind for the past two days.

"Ms. Loveless, are you all right?"

She blinked. "Yes. I—I'm fine."

"You told the police you couldn't give them a description."

She met his unreadable gaze. "You've read the police report. You know that's not what I said." Irritation sharpened her senses. Was he trying to draw her out of the horrible trap of her memories? Or was he hoping to confuse her, to catch her in a lie?

She doubled her hands into fists. "I described the person as medium height, slight build, with a hooded jacket, dark pants and shoes and leather gloves."

"Leather gloves? You didn't mention that before."

Sunny opened her mouth, then closed it. She'd almost said too much. She'd almost told Agent Stone that she'd tasted the leather when the kidnapper had stuffed the note into her mouth.

She shrugged. "Gloves. They smelled like wet leather."

He jotted something in a small spiral pad. "But you couldn't make out any features or distinguishing marks?"

Sunny interlaced her fingers on the tabletop, using all her strength to appear honest and innocent as cold terror enveloped her like the embrace of a ghost.

How long could she fool this self-described expert in missing children? He was asking all the right questions. It was as if he knew.

She *had* noticed a distinguishing feature. Or at least she thought she had.

If she was right, it could be a key to the kidnapper's identity. And if the kidnapper found out Sunny had talked, he would kill Emily.

She kept her eyes on her fingertips. "No. Nothing," she lied. "I couldn't see. The rain was a deluge."

"What did you do then?"

"The store clerk called the police. She stayed with me until the police got there."

The memory of those endless hours and the detective's unrelenting questions sent a shudder through her.

Agent Stone's eyes narrowed, and Sunny's senses immediately went on full alert. She had to stay composed.

"I was soaked," she said lamely.

She could read his mind. He knew she was hiding something. If she were sitting on his side of the table, she'd be thinking the same thing.

He'd probably sat across from a distraught mother or father dozens of times. How many desperate parents had lied to him to protect their children?

Had he already seen through her? She shifted in her seat and the note in her pocket crackled—or was it her guilty imagination?

His eyes never left her face. "You haven't heard anything from the kidnapper? No phone calls? No notes?"

"I've already been through all this," she countered, hearing the tension in her voice. "Why aren't you out there looking for my baby instead of wasting time asking me questions I've already answered?"

"I told you. I need to hear your answers first-hand."

"What's the point? My story is not going to change. I can't tell you where Emily is. Don't you think I wish I could?" Sunny avoided his probing gaze. She didn't like his changeable eyes, or his gruff voice.

"You might be surprised how much you've already told me."

His voice was soothing, encouraging, but the

words sent terror streaking through her. His features were etched with determination. His body telegraphed protection and strength.

God she wanted to trust him. If anyone could help her find her daughter, Sunny believed this man could. If only she dared confide in him. She ducked her head, looking down at her hands. Her knuckles whitened as she squeezed her fingers together, forcing herself to stay strong, to stay silent as his chair scraped on the hardwood floor.

Griff stood and stared at the top of Sunny Loveless's honey-colored head, certainty settling cold and hard beneath his breastbone.

She was gutsier than most women would be in her situation. He had to give her that. But as each moment passed, he became more certain that she'd already heard from the kidnapper.

He stood and walked over to the window. As he brushed by her, a faint fresh scent like the air after a spring shower drifted past his nostrils. Despite his suspicion, despite his resolve, his body responded. He clenched his jaw, forcing himself to picture her wet and bleeding, frantically searching for her daughter in the rain.

He turned in time to see her shoulders tense, and her fingertips tighten around the cup.

He swallowed. She *was* lovely. His gaze traveled over the graceful curve of her back, the fine shape of her head, the honey blond hair twisted up into a messy knot, exposing her delicately curved neck. In another circumstance, he could be attracted to her. Very attracted.

But that would only happen in a different world, a different life. In this one she was hiding information from him, and before he was finished with her she would hate him, because he *would* find her baby. And if that meant he had to bully her or browbeat her, then so be it.

He measured out his life in the tears and smiles of families reunited. A part of his heart died each time he failed to save a child. And there hadn't been that many parts to spare when he'd started with the FBI.

Before he'd left D.C. he'd made himself a promise. He was good at his job, but he knew the taste of failure too well. He was thirty. He'd searched for his sister for fifteen years. That was long enough. It was time to give up on old hopes and move on.

This would be his last missing child case. He would not fail this last time. Not here. He was back home. This time, he would succeed, no matter the cost to him or to the lovely young woman who was deliberately lying to him.

Frustration blossomed into anger in his chest. He stepped in front of her.

"Do you think I haven't seen this before? I know you've been contacted." He glared down at her. "He told you he'd kill her, didn't he?" He sucked in a sharp breath and slapped his open palm on the table. *"Didn't he!"*

She went stone white, and the cup in her hand cracked, spattering coffee all over the table. She jumped up, brown liquid dripping from her fingers.

Griff grabbed a box of tissues and ripped half of them out. He gripped her arm.

"Here." He handed her a wad of tissues, then used the rest to mop up the table.

After he'd tossed the soaked mess toward a trash can, he turned to her.

She stood there valiantly trying to mask the haunted terror that radiated from her pale face as her hands mangled the coffee-stained tissues.

Griff's heart squeezed painfully.

"I'll take that as a yes," he said softly.

Chapter Two

35 hours missing

"I'm a private investigator. Do you think if the kidnapper had contacted me, I would keep it from the police?" Sunny's voice sounded small.

Griff's anger ratcheted up. "I think you'd be more believable if you gave me a straight answer, instead of throwing questions back at me."

She took a long, shaky breath. "If I knew anything that would help you find Emily I'd tell you."

"You're prevaricating. Worse, you're making the assumption that you know better than I do what will help your daughter. I'd like to…" He paused. He'd like to what? Grab her and shake the truth out of her? Or wrap his arms around her and promise her everything would be all right?

Whoa. Where had that thought come from?

He knew too well what an empty promise that

would be. She needed to hear the unvarnished truth. Maybe that would scare her into trusting him.

Her dark green gaze met his, wrenching his heart into a painful knot. He peeled the coffee-stained tissues from her hands and tossed them aside.

"Talk to me, Ms. Loveless." He couldn't bring himself to call her Sunny. The name was too intimate. It brought him too close. He needed distance, detachment. It was the only way he could do this job.

"Tell me the truth. How did they get to you without alerting the police? And more importantly, what do they want?"

The scratches on her cheek flared red against her white skin. Her lower lip trembled slightly. "I never said I'd been contacted."

"Sure you did. With that broken cup and spilled coffee. Do they want money? Did they threaten your daughter's life? That's usual in these cases. I can't help you if you won't talk to me."

She rubbed her palms together, then glanced at her watch. "I don't have time for this. I have to get home. My next-door neighbor Lillian is there alone, trying to piece our case files back together while she waits at a tapped phone in case the kidnapper calls. She's seventy-six, and shouldn't have to shoulder that kind of responsibility by herself."

Despite her effort to be tough, Griff knew she was about to break. "Neither should you. Every moment you delay is a moment off your daughter's life."

He averted his gaze from her shocked, hurt face. Striding over to the window, he thrust his hands into his pockets to hide his clenched fists.

"You think you can deal with these people on your own?" he asked over his shoulder.

Dread certainty filled him. "You're wrong. I've worked with too many distraught parents who thought the same thing. If you don't tell me the truth, your daughter *will* die." His harsh voice echoed through the room.

She made a small, pained sound. "That was cruel, and unnecessary."

"No, it wasn't unnecessary. What's unnecessary is the time you're wasting in this misguided effort to hide the facts from me." He faced her again. "I will not abandon your daughter, Ms. Loveless. I'm going to do my best to find her, with or without your help. I just hope it's not too late."

She raised her head and the fear that racked her shone on her face. "You have to believe me," she said in a choked voice. "If there was anything I could tell you, I would."

In spite of his irritation, Griff almost smiled at her clever wording. "You're smart, Ms. Loveless.

But I'm smart, too. We need to be working together. All kidnappers threaten dire consequences if the family contacts the authorities. The truth is, hearing from the kidnappers is a good sign."

Her brows drew down.

"Once we have contact, we have evidence. It's the ones who grab the baby to keep or sell, the ones who never make contact, that give us nightmares." His gut clenched as his words hung there in the silence.

Nightmares. He knew plenty about nightmares, too. He lived with them on a daily basis. He intended to ensure that this lovely, brave woman wouldn't have to. With or without her help.

Sunny opened her mouth.

He held up his hand. "Spare me another clever turn of phrase that makes you feel better about lying, Ms. Loveless." He flexed his fingers. "I'm going to wash the coffee off my hands. I'll bring you a towel. While I'm gone, you think about *this*. Right now *you* are the biggest obstacle to finding your daughter. If you received a note, you may be destroying DNA evidence. So far, the odds are pretty good that your daughter is safe, because without her, the kidnappers have nothing to bargain with. But no one can guarantee that. The longer Emily is missing, the lower our chances of finding her."

As he stepped past her, her fresh scent teased his nostrils again. She was like a breath of spring to his winter-coated heart.

He was going to have to watch himself around her.

As soon as Agent Stone closed the door, Sunny released the breath she was holding and grabbed her purse. She had to get out of here before he talked her into telling him everything.

She'd been afraid of this when Lieutenant Carver had told her an FBI special agent from Washington, D.C., was being called in.

Griffin Stone knew far too much. His instincts were too good.

It hadn't taken him two minutes to deduce that she was lying. She'd felt his suspicion like a wave of heat.

Worse, his confidence combined with his intimidating presence made her doubt her ability to deal with the kidnapper on her own. She had to get away from him so she could think.

As soon as his footsteps faded, she slipped out of the room and down the fire stairs.

Rubbing her temple where a headache slowly bloomed, she stepped out of the building into the hot summer sun. For an instant, she tilted her head up, inviting the sun's bright heat to penetrate down to her bones.

Not even the sun could thaw her icy heart, though. The fear that had encased it from the instant she'd laid eyes on Emily's empty carrier still chilled her. She would never feel warm or safe again, until her daughter was back in her arms.

Squinting against the sun and her headache, she slung her purse over her shoulder and headed for her car.

As she approached, a patch of white on her windshield caught her eye. It was a scrap of paper, rucked up by the gentle breeze.

She walked faster, her heart thrumming out of rhythm with her quickening strides. Within seconds, its violent pounding sheared her breath.

Was the slip of paper a note from the kidnapper? Information about Emily?

When a couple walking past glanced curiously at her, she realized she was practically running. With a huge effort, she forced herself to slow down. But hope and impatience flared in her chest as she reached out to grab the note.

And froze.

What if the kidnapper was watching her? Or Griffin Stone was peering down at her from the second story? Her mouth went dry. She suppressed the urge to raise her gaze to the window where she'd stood only moments before.

"Just pick it up," she muttered, swallowing anxiously. Was it a ransom note? A joke? Or further instructions from the kidnapper?

Sunny risked a quick glance around her, and what she saw sent a bolt of disappointment thudding into her chest. There were similar slips of paper on most of the cars nearby.

"Oh, no." A moan escaped her lips. It was just some stupid advertising flyer.

She pressed the remote key lock and reached for the door handle as tears clogged her throat. Her baby was out there alone and Sunny was helpless, at the mercy of a faceless threat.

Her eyes went back to her windshield. The paper *was* the same size as the first note, and it appeared to be lined notepaper with a torn edge.

That was no advertising flyer.

She couldn't breathe, couldn't force air past her constricted throat. It was from the kidnapper. She glanced casually around, then looked back toward the building she'd just exited.

She knew how important this evidence was. She knew what she should do. She should leave it there and march back inside and tell Agent Stone about it, so he could examine it and enter it into evidence.

But she couldn't. The block-printed words from the first note appeared in her mind's eye.

Tell the police anything about me and your kid will die.

No. She had only one choice. She plucked the piece of paper from under the windshield wiper with fingers that shook so hard she almost dropped it.

Then she climbed into her car.

Heat enveloped her like a sauna. She swallowed, her throat parched with fearful anticipation. Tension radiated up her neck, intensifying her headache. She turned on the engine, then fished a tissue from her purse and used it to carefully spread the note open on the seat beside her. Agent Stone's warning about destroying DNA echoed in her ears. He was right. She had to preserve the evidence.

More block printing on lined paper. Her scalp tightened. *Just like the first one.*

She struggled to focus her suddenly tear-filled eyes. The words wavered in front of her.

Emily is still alive, for now.

"Oh, thank God!" Sunny's breath whooshed out and a scorching relief swept through her. She clapped a hand over her mouth.

"Emily," she whispered against her fingers as a sense memory caught her off guard. The powdery smell of her daughter's sweet, warm neck, the angel-soft down of her hair. Sunny sucked in a sobbing breath. Then she closed her eyes and released the thick sobs that pressed so hard against her chest. She only allowed herself a few seconds of self-indulgence.

Then she looked back at the note, her vision blurred by tears.

Emily is still alive, for now. But you're spending too much time with the police. Someone you know will be hurt. You'd better point the police in a different direction, or next time, it will be someone you love. Remember, I'm watching you.

"Someone you love…" she whispered, the icy fear taking hold of her again. She shivered, despite the heat.

Oh God! Lil! Had they done something to her dear friend and neighbor? Sunny dug out her cell phone.

The blare of a car horn startled her. She jerked her head up. In her rearview mirror, she saw a car behind her, obviously waiting for her to back out of the parking place. Dazed, she realized she'd been sitting there with her car idling.

Waving an apology at the impatient driver, she backed out and speed-dialed her home number.

Lillian answered on the first ring.

"Lil! Thank God! Are you all right?"

"Of course, darling. Why? Has something happened?"

Sunny took deep, calming breaths. "No. It's nothing. I'll see you in a few minutes."

The impatient driver leaned on the horn again.

She put the car in gear, her throat closing with emotion. Her baby was still alive.

But she couldn't resist cutting her eyes back to the paper lying on the passenger seat. Two words stood out like beacons.

For now.

BY THE TIME Griff returned to the interrogation room, Sunny Loveless had disappeared.

Looking out the window, he'd seen her plunk a piece of paper out from under her windshield wipers. A quick scan of the parking lot told him a lot of other vehicles also had pieces of paper struck on their windshields, too, but his gut told him he'd just watched Sunny Loveless pick up a second message from the kidnapper.

Carver walked in.

"Where's Ms. Loveless?" he asked.

Griff pointed out the window and voiced his suspicion about the note.

"But there's notes on all those cars."

"Yeah. I know." He turned toward the door. "This might be the break we need. Get CSU down there, now, and have men check the side streets and talk to possible witnesses."

"I'll get someone to stop Ms. Loveless and take that note into evidence."

"No. Not yet. Send an unmarked car to make sure no one follows her, and see that she gets home safely. Tell them to stay invisible."

He turned his attention back to Sunny. As he watched, she paused with her foot on the brake, and glanced out her open car window and up toward the second floor. From where he stood he could make out her tortured face and bowed shoulders. Her jerky movements telegraphed her pain.

She was wondering if he'd seen her take the note.

He considered sprinting downstairs to her car and stopping her. With very little effort, he could force her to give him the note.

But what if whoever had left it was watching her? The last thing Griff wanted to do was put her or her baby in more danger. So he decided to wait until he figured out just what she was hiding.

He'd visit her at her home later, after he'd had a chance to review the specific case files that had been taken in the break-in.

This kidnapping was a puzzle. Ms. Loveless didn't have the kind of money that attracted kidnappers. Her adopted daughter's mother, Brittany, was a high school senior. The father was a construction worker who was subsequently imprisoned for statutory rape. He'd been released two months earlier, and had tried to contact Brittany, but her mother had called the police. Carver was checking on his whereabouts now.

In fact, Carver had detectives following up on all of Loveless Inc.'s cases, most of which had turned out just as advertised—with happy endings. Carver himself was checking out the three vaguely threatening phone calls Loveless Inc.'s published number had received since the break-in.

So if the kidnappers didn't want money, or revenge, what did they want? If Griff wasn't so certain Sunny had been contacted, he'd think the baby had been stolen by one of the numerous emotionally disturbed women who snatch a baby to keep for their own.

After she'd pulled out of the parking lot, he bounded out of the room and made quick work of the service stairs. When he burst through the fire door and out into the parking lot, he stepped over to a nearby car and grabbed the note stuck beneath its windshield wiper. He looked at it.

The paper was blank.

Gravel crunched as Carver walked up beside him.

"I'll be a son of a gun." Carver's deep voice boomed. "There's nothing on it. Not one word."

Griff crushed the paper in his fist as he looked around at the other cars.

"I've got CSU coming. So you were right. The kidnapper was in our parking lot, right under our noses."

Griff flipped the paper over. Nothing on the other side, either. "Somebody was."

"What do you think they want? Ransom?"

"This doesn't feel like a kidnapping for ransom. I'm afraid that in one of her hearts-and-flowers investigations, Ms. Loveless uncovered something damaging about someone. Something they're desperate to keep hidden."

"Well, if that's so, why not go after her directly? Why steal her baby? Taking care of a baby ain't easy."

Griff nodded. "It puts the abductors in a dangerous position, too. Few things are more noticeable than an infant."

Nauseating fear suddenly filled him. They

could keep Sunny hanging on for a long time by telling her the child was safe.

As if reading his mind, Carver said, "If they took the baby just to keep Ms. Loveless quiet about something…"

Griff nodded grimly. "There's no guarantee the child survived the first night. Emily may already be dead."

"WHAT'S THE MATTER?" Lillian jumped to her feet behind Loveless Inc.'s reception desk the moment Sunny opened the front door. With a huge effort, Sunny kept her face composed, acutely conscious of the police officer who was trying to blend with the shadows on the west side of the foyer, just a few feet from where they stood.

"Nothing." Sunny swallowed. "How are the files coming?"

Lillian's sharp brown eyes assessed her. "I'm about half finished reviewing our backup disks, trying to recreate the files. Just a little while ago, the police finally brought back *copies* of the paper files that weren't stolen. They're still combing through the originals."

"Nice to know it took having my daughter kidnapped to make them pay attention to the break-in."

Lil's thin lips curled upward. "It's how they

have to work, hon. They concentrate on the dangerous cases, and get to the others when they can."

Sunny bit her trembling lip. "I know, but if I'd made a bigger fuss about the break-in, maybe Emily wouldn't have been taken."

"Don't do that to yourself. The computer technician told me they'd concluded that the thief was after information. Otherwise why take the paper files and wipe the hard drive? They could easily have walked out with the entire computer."

"Wow, that's brilliant. And it's exactly what I told the officers the night of the break-in." Anger pushed away Sunny's haze of panic.

"You need some tea. Come on." Lillian held out her hand.

Sunny stepped around the desk and let her next-door neighbor lead her through the archway into the living room, and on into the kitchen. Two years ago, when Sunny had moved into this house and started her detective agency, Lillian had appointed herself Sunny's assistant. She claimed that since she'd retired from her job as an IRS investigator, she wasn't getting any "action," as she'd put it.

The afternoon sun shining through the trees drew changing patterns on the tile floor as Sunny slipped into a chair. From where she sat, the polished wood of Emily's high chair gleamed cheerily.

She propped her elbows on the wooden table and put her face in her hands.

"I know something else has happened," Lillian said in a low voice as she set a cup of tea in front of Sunny. "Did the FBI agent have any news?"

"No." Sunny pushed her fingers through her hair. Then, using a napkin, she fished the note from her pocket and spread it on the table.

Lillian put a hand to her throat. "Oh, my God, a second note?"

"Read it," Sunny said, hunching her stiff shoulders.

Lillian did, then looked up, her lined face pale. "Where did you find this?"

"On the windshield of my car. Right there in the police parking lot in broad daylight. He *knew* I was talking to the police. He surely knows the FBI has been called in." She wrapped her hands around the warm cup. "Why won't he tell me what he wants?"

Lillian read the words aloud.

"Emily is still alive, for now. But you're spending too much time with the police. Someone you know will be hurt. You'd better point the investigation in a different direction, or next time, it will be someone you love. Remember, I'm watching you."

She looked up.

Sunny met her gaze. "I was afraid they'd hurt you."

"Don't you worry about me. I can take care of myself. I still have a few tricks up my sleeve from my IRS investigator days. It's you I'm worried about."

Sunny sent her friend a weary smile. "It was the luckiest day of my life when I moved next door to you."

Lillian smiled back at her, but her smile faded quickly. "Sunny, you have to show the police the notes."

"What? How can I? This is the second time this monster has threatened to kill Emily. Now he's threatening to hurt people I know. He knows every move I make. And so far I haven't told the police anything. If I turn over the notes now—"

"The police and the FBI are used to dealing with kidnappers. They have resources I can't tap into. Their DNA index—CODIS. And AFIS, the fingerprint database. I know you're trying to be careful with the evidence, but what good is preserving it if you're not going to give it to the police to examine and test?"

Aghast, Sunny stared at Lillian. "What if the notes lead them to the kidnapper? What then? What if the police and the FBI start closing in on him?" She tried to swallow, but her throat was dry as sand. "He'll know I told them about him. He will *kill* her," she croaked.

Lillian's face reflected both sympathy and sadness. "Darling, every kidnapper warns the family not to contact the police. You know that. What would you tell your client to do?"

"This is not an ordinary kidnapping. It's obvious from the messages that Emily was taken because of something I stumbled into. I don't know what, yet. But if the police can trace these people through the notes, then so can I, with your help. Meanwhile, I can't tell anyone anything. They're *watching* me."

"This is *not* different. It's exactly the same as your other cases. Every minute that passes, Emily is in more danger. You know I'll help you. But we can't do this alone. You have to give the notes to the FBI."

Lillian's words stabbed Sunny's heart like a knife. Her last ally, her friend, had turned against her.

"I *KNEW* JANIE WAS LYING!" Bess Raymond stopped in the middle of undressing the baby girl and looked up at the television. The twenty-four hour news channel was following up on an AMBER Alert that had been issued in Nashville, Tennessee, almost forty-eight hours before. "She said you came from Cleveland. But she was too antsy. Too nervous. She stole you in Nashville, right back where she started." She shook her head in wonder. "Nashville…"

"Emily Rose Loveless, six-month-old daughter of Sunny Loveless, was abducted Tuesday night—"

The news anchor's voice pulled her back to the present moment. "Did you hear that, Emily Rose?" Bess cooed. "That's you." She shook her head. "Janie's clever, but she can be really stupid. It never even occurred to her to check you for identification." She tickled Emily under the chin. "If she had, she'd have found the ID bracelet on your ankle. It was probably too big for your little wrist, wasn't it?"

The baby giggled as Bess tickled her foot.

The delicate piece of gold jewelry that had been hidden by the baby's ruffled socks now rested in Bess's leather logbook in the bottom drawer of her ancient desk. It had the name EMILY ROSE LOVELESS engraved on the front, and a telephone number on the back.

"Sunny Loveless, a private investigator whose detective agency, Loveless, Inc., advertises happy endings for its clients, can only wait, hoping for her own happy ending."

Bess looked up from changing Emily's diaper in time to see a shot of a pretty Victorian house with a wooden sign over the door.

When she had Emily snugly dressed in a footed sleeper, she tucked her back into her carrier.

"Oh Emily Rose, now we know where you came from. You live in that pretty house we saw on TV in Nashville. I should have recognized the area code of your phone number."

The screen changed to a long shot of a young woman with honey-gold hair being guided into the house by an older woman. "Look, sweetie. There's your mommy. She must be missing you so much."

Emily started to whine.

"I know you want to see her. I'll have your bottle all ready in just a minute."

She bent over the bottom drawer of the desk, digging out the worn leather notebook where she had recorded every baby that had come through her home. She reverently opened it to the first page.

"Almost fifteen years to the day," she whispered, touching the notation written there in her own neat script. Fifteen years ago Janie had shown up with the first child—an adorable toddler who'd become Bess's daughter, filling the awful void left by the death of her own child. Her lips turned up in a sad smile. Mia was so grown-up now. She'd be going to college in the fall.

Her heart filled to bursting with love for her beautiful daughter, but it broke every time she looked at the book, every time she thought about Mia's real family and how they must have suffered all these years.

She turned page after page. So many children. So much happiness—so much heartache.

"I think fifteen years is long enough. Don't you, Emily Rose? Enough stolen children. Enough heartbroken families."

Emily gurgled. Bess picked up the engraved silver rattle she'd found buried in Emily's carrier and jiggled it in front of her face. The baby squealed happily, waving her arms.

"Time for Old Bess to come clean. A lot of people deserve to know the truth. Including my own daughter."

Anxiety and loss stabbed through her. She'd been such a coward. She'd never told Mia all the details of her adoption. Mia would hate her when she found out Bess had kept stolen children for

Janie. That Mia herself had been stolen from her family.

"But that's okay." Tears wound their way down her weathered cheeks. "I had her this long. I love her as much as if I'd given birth to her, just like your mommy loves you. I guess I always knew it would end one day."

Sniffing, Bess turned to the last page, where she had carefully recorded Emily's information.

Cleveland, Ohio. Emily Rose Loveless. June twenty-first.

She crossed out Cleveland and wrote in *Nashville*.

"Janie didn't want me to know she'd been back to Nashville, where all this started." She tickled Emily's chin and was rewarded with a toothless smile.

"I can't let her get away with this again. There's been too much heartache already." She raised her chin.

Determination flared inside her as she secured the delicate anklet between the pages of the notebook, then pushed it back down into the drawer, beneath a stack of papers.

"That should be hidden well enough." Bess picked up Emily and bounced her on her lap as she reached for the bottle. "Emily, don't tell anyone where that book is, okay?" She chuckled. "If anyone ever gets their hands on it, I'll go to prison. Now here's your bottle. Isn't that good? You're such a little sweetheart. You'll see your mommy soon. I promise." She shifted the small weight in her arms. "Tomorrow evening, we'll go for a drive, and find a pay phone to call from, so the police can't trace us."

Bess nodded to herself. Janie had never come back for a baby inside of a week. She liked to make sure everything was set up before she had to pick up the child.

She shook her head. "God forbid Janie should be bothered with a baby herself for even one day."

She tried to ignore the small voice that kept warning her that something was different about this child. Janie hadn't been acting like her usual cool-as-a-cucumber self.

She'd been agitated. What if she came back early? Or called while Bess and Emily were gone? What if she found out what Bess was planning to do? Janie was ruthless. Bess had no doubt Janie could provide evidence that would put Bess in jail and leave Janie in the clear.

That didn't matter. Bess held out a finger and Emily Rose grasped it trustingly. Bess's eyes filled with tears.

The only thing that mattered was this child, and all the other children.

Janie's baby stealing was about to stop.

46 hours missing

HIRAM COGBURN KNOCKED on apartment number one. The foyer of the old house on a backstreet near Vanderbilt University had two apartments downstairs and two upstairs. He remembered it from back in the day, when Ed and Janie had lived upstairs in apartment number four.

A twinge of irritation cramped his ample belly. It soured his stomach to think about how his old law school buddy had ended up in the money and was running for the New York State Legislature, while Hiram was reduced to chasing ambulances and advertising on cable for DUI cases. Life just wasn't fair.

When he'd gotten the call from Ed's crazy wife, telling him she needed his help diverting a private investigator's attention from Ed, Hiram had refused to get involved. But Janie had threatened him with exposure if he didn't help her. *Ed's future is at stake,* she'd told him.

As if he cared.

He'd reminded her that for every illegal act he'd committed, she'd done a dozen, but then she'd mentioned a dollar amount that had set his mouth to watering.

Still, it was a tough decision. He'd always liked Ed, but Janie Gross scared the spit out of him. She was nuts. There was no predicting what she would do if he pissed her off enough.

Her final words on the phone still rang in his ears. *I'll squash you like a bug, Hiram, and you know I can do it.* She was right. He knew.

Still, he needed the money. And Janie was clever. She wanted Sunny Loveless off their scent, and she'd planned the break-in at the investigator's office to take care of that. Hiram had mined Loveless's case files for ideas to distract her from Ed and Janie. He made mysterious threatening phone calls, pretending to be disgruntled clients or injured parties from her recent cases.

It was working, too. Loveless hadn't contacted the Grosses again.

But Janie couldn't leave well enough alone. She'd come to Nashville to check on Hiram, and ended up stealing Sunny Loveless's baby. Now Hiram was in too deep to get out.

He knocked again.

The fellow who opened the door looked eighty-five if he was a day.

Hiram flashed his fake badge and smiled at him.

"Good evening." He paused for effect, like the cops did on TV. He liked playing a detective. It made him feel important.

"Mr. Joseph Mabry? Hate to bother you so late. We just need a few minutes more of your time. Need to straighten out a few things."

"Police yesterday and twice today? I told that detective this afternoon that y'all know everything I know."

The police had been here this afternoon? Hiram swallowed nervously. "Uh, we're all pitching in on this case. You know how it is when a kid goes missing."

Why had the police come back here today? Had Loveless told them something else? His stomach churned. "Well, I just need to confirm a couple of things. Now, how long ago did Ms. Loveless first contact you?"

"Month or so ago. She said she was looking for someone named Jane from back around '91. I told her everything I remembered about Ed Gross and his wife. I'd plumb forgot about those two until Ms. Loveless showed up asking all those questions. Hell, I hardly ever saw Ed Gross, and that wife of his was more scarce than him. She never stuck her nose out the door. The police think they stole the Loveless woman's baby?"

Hiram took a ragged envelope and a stubby pencil from his pocket. "We're looking at all Ms. Loveless's cases. Trying to eliminate suspects in the disappearance of her baby. You know how it is. She mentioned your name in her police report."

"Right. She said there were four Janes that she was trying to track down. Looking for her client's birth parents." Mabry squinted at him. "Say, haven't I seen you before?"

"Nope. I just need to see the apartment where they stayed."

The old man sighed and looked behind him, toward the pallid blue light flickering in the darkness. "Awright, but can we hurry? I'm watching *Law & Order.*"

Hiram followed him up the stairs.

Talk to him, Janie had said when she'd seen Mabry's name in the Loveless woman's case file on Jennifer Curry. *Make sure he hasn't told the police anything. If he remembers me being pregnant, or the day we left town, he could ruin us all. He's got to be ninety, so he probably doesn't remember how to pee, but I can't take that chance.*

At the top of the stairs, the old man was hardly out of breath. Hiram, on the other hand, was wheezing. He hitched up his pants and wiped his face with a handkerchief.

"So, it's real sad, her baby being stolen, isn't it?" Hiram struggled for breath.

"Yep. Real sad. She was a nice young lady. The Grosses stayed in apartment number four." Mabry pointed a gnarled finger at a door that was tucked in behind the stairwell. "I can't let you inside. It's rented. Summer students. Mostly the apartments are empty this time of year."

"Then why'd you drag me up here?" Hiram huffed, struggling to catch his breath. "You could have told me that downstairs."

"You're the one who said you wanted to see the apartment. Them other detectives were interested in how the door's hidden by the stairs."

"Right, right." Hiram tucked his handkerchief back in his pocket.

"I told Ms. Loveless I thought the wife was in the family way, but it was hard to tell. She stayed to herself and always wore them baggy dresses. But I never did see a baby. Then they up and left June 30, '91. Just disappeared in the night."

"You remember the exact day they left?" Hiram hadn't remembered. All he knew was, he and Ed had been job hunting together, up until the day he'd come by to pick up Ed and discovered they were gone. Surprised the hell out of him. And scared him, truth be told. He hadn't slept for weeks, afraid the police were going to show up on his doorstep.

He'd have bet his right arm that skipping town had been Janie's idea. He'd never liked Janie. She'd always been weird, and ruthless. He wouldn't have put it past her to turn him in for his part in their baby-selling racket. He'd been petrified that he'd go down alone. Nothing ever seemed to touch Janie. It was as if she were invisible.

"Tell me, Mr. Mabry. Did you mention the date they left to the police?"

"More'n likely."

The date was the one thing Janie was so worried about. Hiram had wondered why, until he'd spent a day searching through the newspaper archives, reading every news story from that day fifteen years ago. One story in particular had caught his eye, the story of the disappearance of a toddler from a public space, and suddenly it all made sense. He understood why Janie was so worried.

It was nice, having something on her for a change. Maybe she'd pay him more, when she found out how much he knew.

He knew the truth. Still, if he could find the answer that easily, then so could Sunny Loveless. So could the police. It would be obvious why Ed and Janie had fled town so abruptly. If Loveless had put the when and the why together, and if she'd told the police, Ed and Janie would be toast. And Hiram knew they'd take him down with them.

"Are we done now?"

Hiram shook his head, making a show of writing on the envelope. "Just a couple more questions. How is it you remember the exact date?"

"Why, 'cause their rent was due on the first of the month. They skipped out on me the night before." He shook his head. "First time I ever had a tenant skip out on me. I'll never forget it."

Mabry shuffled over to the stairs and put his hand on the banister. "I gotta get back downstairs. I'm missing *Law & Order*. The original. That's my favorite."

The old man squinted at him. "You sure look familiar. You never lived here—I'd remember that. But you've been around before."

Hiram shook his head. "Not me. I guess I've just got one of those faces."

"Nope. I know I've seen you before. Right around the time the Grosses lived here. Let me see that badge again."

"I'm telling you you're wrong."

"And I'm telling you I never forget a face."

Hiram felt sweat running down the side of his

neck and pooling at the base of his spine. He couldn't afford to have the old man recognize him. He needed to get out of here.

"Well, you forgot this one. I hate that you had to miss *Law & Order.*" He put out a hand, his heart pounding like a jackhammer. Old men tripped and fell downstairs all the time, didn't they? "Here. Let me give you a hand."

Chapter Three

59 hours missing

The next morning Griff slammed the door of his rental car and lifted his gaze to the brick Victorian house with its white gingerbread molding. In the early-morning sunlight it looked elegant and lovely and proud, just like its owner.

A small wood-burned sign hung over the entrance. Loveless, Inc. We Specialize in Happy Endings.

The ache in his chest grew. He ran his palm across his breastbone and took a deep breath.

What would Sunny have to say about happy endings once he told her about the suspicious death Carver had called him about at three o'clock this morning?

Walking up to the front door, he rang the doorbell.

A man of medium height in a wrinkled sport coat opened the door.

Griff showed him his badge. "Griff Stone, FBI."

The man pulled his coat back to reveal his Nashville Police Department badge. "The Lieutenant told me you might show up."

He stepped back and Griff strode past him into the foyer. A staircase faced a bay window on his right; there was a closed door on the left wall, and a tall doorway arched ten feet in front of him.

In the doorway between the foyer and the living room, a Queen Anne table served as a reception desk, and behind the table sat a slender elderly lady in a bright pink jogging suit. She had a phone propped between her shoulder and chin and was typing rapidly on a computer keyboard.

"Yes, Mr. Thomas, that's right. As long as you continue to pay your child support, you can claim the deductions." Her mouth pursed with disgust as she listened.

Griff let his gaze roam the reception area. It was clean and bright, with gauzy curtains at the windows and family photographs on the walls.

Several of the photos were of Ms. Loveless with a beautiful, fair-skinned baby with downy blond hair. The kidnapped child. He'd seen a newspaper clipping, but now he quickly studied the infant's features. His gaze took in Ms. Loveless's happy smile and the brilliant emerald sparkle in her eyes as she held her child. His heart twisted.

"Fine then," the woman at the desk said briskly. "The IRS thanks you."

As Griff turned, she hit Enter on her keyboard with a flourish and hung up the phone. "Deadbeat piece of scum," she muttered.

Griff cocked an eyebrow. "The IRS?"

The lady shrugged as she briefly met his gaze, her eyes twinkling. "I used to be an investigator. The lingo comes in handy if I need some information."

She dropped her gaze to his shoes. As she panned his pants legs to his belt, then on up, he felt as if he was being measured for something—possibly a coffin.

"You must be the FBI agent. If you were a local, I'd remember you."

"I'm Special Agent Griffin Stone."

The lady's sharp brown eyes snapped to his face. Her eyebrows lifted a couple of millimeters. "You have ID?"

He held it out. "And you are?"

She glanced down at his badge and ID card, then back up at him. "Lillian Jackson. Next-door neighbor, friend, assistant. What can I do for you, Mr. Stone?"

"I need to see Ms. Loveless. It's important."

The lady's face changed and she clutched her collar. "Is it Emily? Did you find her?"

"No ma'am. Sorry. But I need to discuss some things with Sunny, ask her some questions."

The lady looked toward the staircase. "She's not up yet. She hasn't slept since Tuesday night. I'm intimately familiar with the case. Perhaps I can help you."

"Not with this. I need to talk to her," he said. "Now."

Lillian sat up, shaking her head.

"It's okay, Lil. I'm awake."

The hoarse, soft voice floated down to Griff. He lifted his gaze.

She'd descended a few steps down the staircase, far enough to see his face.

She was dressed in a loose white T-shirt and pajama bottoms that were blue with white clouds. Her body was as slender and curvaceous as he'd imagined it under the tailored slacks and shirt she'd worn yesterday, with the same airbrushed skin he remembered. The scratches on her cheek seemed a little fainter.

"Is it about Emily?" The hope that lifted her voice and sparkled in her eyes was heartbreaking. He hated to quash it.

He shook his head. "No, but it is relevant to the case."

The sparkle went out of her eyes, and for Griff, the day turned less bright.

She nodded. "I'll be down as soon as I dress."

"Are you sure, darling?" Lillian asked with a frown. "I know you didn't sleep well."

"I'm okay." She walked back up the stairs, and Griff watched her bare feet and slender ankles until they disappeared at the top of the stairs. He swallowed. He'd never paid any attention to a woman's feet before.

He turned to find a sad smile lighting Lillian's face.

"She's been so brave. Emily has been her whole life for the past six months. The courage you see is just a front. Inside, she's about to fall apart." Love and worry rang in Lillian's voice.

He nodded. "Yes, ma'am. Ms. Jackson, what do you know about her cases, her friends, her enemies? Who would want to hurt her?"

Lillian sank deeper into her chair and assessed him keenly.

He waited.

"Most of the people she's helped send Christmas cards, with pictures of their kids and pets. I could probably count unhappy clients on one hand."

"Maybe you could do that for me."

Lillian Jackson brushed a strand of gray hair

away from her face. "Lately, there have been some harassing phone calls, a couple of different people—I think."

"Like your deadbeat piece of scum on the phone just now?"

She nodded. "His ex-wife hired Sunny to find him. He was using his child support to vacation in Jamaica with his girlfriend. When Sunny tracked him down, he told her she'd be sorry she'd meddled in his life."

Griff flipped his notebook open and skimmed his notes. "Would that be Bob Thomas? He has an alibi for Tuesday night."

Lillian nodded. "I know."

"So you just called him to harass him?"

"And to get a record of his voice. We've been trying to put all our case files back together since the break-in a month and a half ago. Someone has called a couple of times making vague threats about stopping Sunny's meddling, but I don't think it was him."

His mouth quirked. "Says the IRS investigator?"

She straightened. "That's right."

"Then who could it be?"

"The first one that comes to mind, of course, is Burt Means."

"Means?" Griff flipped pages in his note-book. "The father?"

"Right. Emily's biological father. Sunny helped prosecute him for statutory rape. He threatened her."

"And his release from prison fits the timeline. Anyone else?"

"A man who wanted to find the sister he hadn't seen for ten years. She didn't want to see him. Got really angry at Sunny."

"What about others?"

Lillian nodded at his notebook. "Don't you have them all in there?"

Griff cocked his brow. "Yes, I do, but a written report is never as good as an interview."

"That's certainly true."

Griff held her gaze. "Ms. Jackson, you of all people know the importance of having all the facts."

Lillian's gaze turned wary.

Griff leaned over the desk and stared into her eyes. "You know she's got to give us the notes. She's putting her baby in grave danger by hiding her contact with the kidnappers. I saw her find the note yesterday."

He waited, holding his breath, while she assessed him. Did she know about the notes? And if she did, which side would win—her logical investigator side, or the protective, mothering side?

"Sunny's so tired, and she's been through so much."

He didn't answer.

Finally she sighed. "I've tried to reason with her." Her eyes glistened damply. "She's not thinking like a private investigator. She's thinking like a mother."

Griff nodded and straightened. A strong-willed mother. With more guts than most. He straightened. Maybe now she'd listen to reason. Now that tragedy had struck.

WHEN THE PHONE RANG, Hiram shot straight up in bed. His heart leaped into his throat. It rang again, pumping fear through his veins like blood.

It was the police. He knew it was.

He'd fallen into bed fully clothed after cowering in his apartment all night, sweating like a pig, hardly able to breathe as he waited for the knock on the door he was sure he'd hear any second.

He'd never moved as fast in his life as when he'd scrambled down those stairs and past the ominously still body of Mabry, crumpled on the bottom step.

The phone kept ringing. Hiram looked at it, wishing the thing would just explode into pieces and leave him alone.

With a hand that shook like an old man, he gingerly lifted the receiver to his ear.

"What the hell have you done?"

Janie's strident voice scraped across his nerves like a cheese grater against bare knuckles. Wincing, thinking he might be better off in the hands of the police, he opened his mouth.

But all that emerged was a pathetic, unmanly squeak.

"Hiram, you—" Janie let loose with a string of invectives that would make a longshoreman blush.

He swung his legs onto the floor and tried to get up, but his knees were like jelly. "Janie," he croaked.

"—complete and utter idiot." Finally she ran out of steam.

He heard her draw deeply on a cigarette.

"I don't know what happened." He remembered thinking about pushing Mabry, then suddenly the old man was lying ominously still at the foot of the stairs.

"You don't—how can you not know? I'm sitting here watching the *national* news and hearing that the landlord of the apartment where Eddie and I lived fell down his stairs. He's *dead*. How in the hell does that divert attention, you incompetent, blubbering fool?"

"It was an accident. I can fix it."

"Fix it?" Janie yelled, then coughed. "How?"

Hiram tried again to rise. His knees held, so he stood and paced, raking his hand through his thinning hair. He had no clue, but he would never admit that to her.

Think!

"The father!" he blurted. The lump that choked his throat made his voice squeaky. "Burt Means just got out of prison. The Loveless woman put him there. He was a construction worker. I'll rig something to scare 'em, and leave a clue to link it to him."

"Hang on, hang on. Let me think."

Hiram grimaced at the sound of Janie hacking through the phone. He walked over to the window and lifted the dusty blinds just enough to peer out.

What if he'd left something at the landlord's place? He broke out in a cold sweat. Where was the damn envelope he'd been writing on?

"You cannot screw this up, Hiram. If I have to come down there and take care of things again, I'll take care of you at the same time. Do you understand me?"

"D-don't worry. I'll come up with something."

"No. Please. Do *not* come up with anything. You listen to me. Do it this way."

Hiram listened, wiping a sheen of sweat off his face. The lump in his throat finally began to dissolve.

He had to hand it to Janie—she was a nut, but she was a smart nut.

SUNNY DID NOT WANT to have to deal with Griffin Stone again. He read her much too easily. She was used to being the one who slipped in under other people's defenses. She didn't like having the tables turned.

She halted at the dining room door. In the sun-filled kitchen, he stood with his back to her, accepting a cup of coffee from Lillian.

He wore a lightweight navy-blue sport coat and creased khaki slacks, with classic penny loafers. His dark hair teased the collar of his shirt. As he reached to take the coffee, the subtle movement of his shoulders inside the jacket drew her eye. They were broad shoulders, strong shoulders. They looked as if they could carry a heavy burden with ease.

Sunny swallowed the lump of fear and loneliness that briefly clogged her throat. She took a deep breath, lifted her chin and walked into the kitchen.

"Here she is," Lillian said. "Darling, do you want coffee?"

Agent Stone turned, and Sunny saw his eyes in full light for the first time. She suppressed a gasp. They were a deep blue-violet, possibly the most beautiful eyes she'd ever seen. Surrounded by black lashes and topped by straight dark brows, they softened his strong, harshly planed face.

"Um, yes, thanks, Lil. I'd like some."

She sat at the kitchen table, gesturing for the agent to sit too, but he waited until Lillian had poured one more cup of coffee.

After Lillian set the cup in front of her, she touched Sunny on the shoulder. "I'm going home for a while. I have laundry to do and some other chores. The officer up front can answer the phone." Lillian briefly glanced toward Griff. "Unless you need me here?"

Sunny shook her head. "No. I'm fine."

Lillian's hand cupped Sunny's chin. "I hope you gave some thought to what I said yesterday. It would be so much easier for you." Lillian kissed her cheek. "Nice to meet you, Agent Stone."

"Call me Griff, ma'am." Griff nodded at her. "Good to meet you, too."

Lillian smiled warmly at him. "Griff," she said.

After Lillian left, he pulled out a chair and sat across from Sunny. "So here we are again, on opposite sides of the table."

His voice was distressingly cheerful.

She rubbed her temple, then sipped her coffee, grimacing at its bitter taste. Everything tasted like ashes, and would, she knew, until Emily was back home with her.

"You said you had information relevant to my daughter's case?" she asked coldly.

He pulled a torn piece of lined notepaper from his pocket.

Sunny almost dropped her cup. It clattered against the wooden tabletop.

"Wh-where did you get that?" she stammered, terror streaking through her.

"From a car windshield in the precinct parking lot. You have one just like it. I watched you pick it up yesterday afternoon."

Adrenaline sizzled through her veins. Her pulse jackhammered. She'd known he was watching her, even though she'd tried to deny it. She'd felt his burning stare.

He held the piece of paper between two fingers, as if taunting her with it. She met his gaze briefly, but her eyes kept going back to the paper. What did the other notes have on them? It hadn't occurred to her to wonder that until now.

"Is it a flyer?"

"You know it's not." He spread the sheet out in front of her. It was blank. "Turn it over."

His voice held a command she couldn't refuse. She reached out with a hand that shook, and nudged the paper over. Her breath caught. "There's nothing on it."

Relief and fear collided in her chest. Relief

that he didn't *know* her sheet was not blank, and fear that he was about to somehow trick her into admitting she'd gotten another note.

She wiped her hand with her napkin and waited, looking down at her cup, dreading his next words.

"But there was writing on yours, wasn't there? I saw how you reacted. I watched you read it. Show me the note, Ms. Loveless."

She reached for her cup, trying for casual, but her hand shook so much she gave up the effort and balled it into a fist.

He surprised her by leaning forward and covering her hand with his. His skin was warm, his fingers hard and strong, like the rest of him, like his name.

His hand was much larger than hers, but it looked graceful and competent. She had no doubt he could break a neck or hold a baby with equal care and skill.

Her vision grew hazy as she imagined letting him take the burden from her shoulders. He might be cool and *just-the-facts,* but he exuded a confidence Sunny craved.

"You don't know what you're asking," she whispered. She bit her tongue so the answers he sought wouldn't slip out. She felt like a rabbit caught in headlights—paralyzed with fear. Yet she had to make a decision. She didn't know which way to turn for safety.

As if she'd spoken aloud, he answered her. "My expertise is in child abductions. So trust me, I do know. I've had cases like this before."

"Not like this one." She pulled her hand from under his. His touch was too reassuring, too tempting. It made her want to trust him.

Her throat closed up and it took her a moment to speak. "Have you ever had a case with a baby this small? Emily is only six months old."

He nodded. "Often when—"

She interrupted him. "Did you get the baby back?"

"Ms. Loveless—"

"Did you?"

A shadow crossed his face, and Sunny's heart sank. She'd almost let him convince her that he could make everything right.

But this wasn't a fairy tale and Griffin Stone was no knight in shining armor. He was just a human being with human failings. One more obstacle between her and the most important thing in her life—her child, Emily.

"Children are most often taken by a relative," he said. "Most are returned to their family safe and sound. I've handled eleven child abductions with the FBI. Five were children younger than one year. Four of those were taken by a family member. All four were eventually recovered. The fifth infant was taken by a stranger."

He raised his gaze to hers, his incredible eyes hooded and dark.

Sunny's shoulders ached with tension. "And—?"

He shook his head. The faint lines around his mouth deepened. "That was three years ago. We never found him. He's still listed as missing."

Through numb lips, Sunny said, "This is not a family member abduction."

He didn't speak.

"And it's not some deranged woman who wants a baby for herself."

His face softened, although his eyes didn't. "I know."

Her heart lurched painfully. Hearing him confirm her fears frightened her even more. If the kidnapper wasn't a family member or a stranger, then what did that mean for Emily's safety?

"I keep thinking if I hadn't adopted Emily, she'd be safe now. She'd be with a stable, loving, protective family." She took a shaky breath. "Or if I'd only waited to go to the store. I didn't have to have milk—"

"You can go insane thinking about all the *if onlies*." His voice was rough with some emotion. "Don't keep piling more guilt onto yourself.

You'll collapse. And that won't do your daughter any good. Give me the notes. Let me help you."

Her shoulders ached, her head pounded. She looked up at him, searching his eyes for a peek into his soul.

He sat there without moving, allowing her in for an instant. And in that instant she'd caught a glimpse of a sadness so profound it hurt her heart.

She moistened her lips and asked quietly, "Why do you do it?"

The sadness expanded, drew her in, until she felt consumed by it. On some deep visceral level he understood her pain.

Then he blinked and just like that, he withdrew.

"It's a job," he said dismissively. "I'm good at it."

Sunny shook her head, still holding his gaze. "That can't be why."

He looked down at his cup. "That's the best explanation I have. Now, are you going to make me get a search warrant for those notes?"

She tried to swallow, but her throat was too dry. "What about the other children?"

He frowned up at her.

"The other six cases you handled."

His eyes flickered, looked past her for an instant before returning to her face. "Those children were older. I thought you were interested in infants."

"I'm interested in your record."

He straightened, almost imperceptibly, as if he were bracing himself. "Four were recovered safe and sound. The other two—"

Suddenly, the memory of a recent news story surfaced in Sunny's mind. She blinked. "Oh, my God, you were the agent on the case of that Senator's son, weren't you?"

He didn't answer, but she saw the self-recrimination in his suddenly stoic features, in the slight wavering of his gaze.

Details of the case came back to her in a rush. "Didn't the boy's father pay the ransom? He didn't go to the police." Fear sheared her breath. The Senator had thought he could handle the kidnappers himself.

"What happened?" she asked anxiously. "Why did the boy end up dead?"

Griff shook his head. "We were too late. The kidnappers fled as soon as they got their money. They never revealed the boy's final location. By the time we found him, he had died of exposure."

"So, you're saying that if the Senator had called in the police sooner—"

"No. The child's safety was my responsibility."

"But if you'd been called in earlier you'd have had a better chance."

"Most of the time it's the best course of action."

He leveled his gaze on her. "The most difficult infant abduction cases are the ones where the person wants the baby for themselves. Often those children are never found."

Emotion roughened his voice. "The most dangerous are the cases where the baby is used as leverage or for revenge."

He paused, and Sunny's breath stuck in her throat.

"That's what I think this is."

"Leverage?" she croaked.

He nodded. "You have something they want. And they're desperate to get it. You can't deal with these people alone. You have to trust someone to help you." Griff's eyes probed hers. "Trust me."

Tears filled her eyes and overflowed. His words, his eyes, called to her. *Share the burden. Let me help you.*

"They said they would kill her."

Griff nodded solemnly. "I know."

"But you might be too late." She didn't say *again* but she knew he heard it in her voice.

He winced and closed his eyes briefly. He touched her hand. "I promise you, I will die if that's what it takes to save your daughter."

The absolute conviction in his voice stunned her. *I will die.*

She couldn't move. All she could do was stare at his hand, so large against her smaller, paler one.

Finally she made a fist, then pulled away and pressed her knuckles against her lips.

"Why?"

He looked up at her, startled. "Why what?"

"Why would you die to save her?"

He swallowed and his jaw clenched. "I told you, it's my job."

She shook her head in denial. He wasn't just a man doing his job. For whatever reason, this was personal.

"I'm so afraid."

"I know."

"They said they would kill her. How can I just ignore that?"

"I swear I will get your daughter back."

The determination in his face was unmistakable. His violet eyes burned with fervor.

"I would, too."

His brow furrowed. "Would what?"

"I would die if it meant Emily would be safe."

A wry smile tilted one corner of his mouth. "Then we agree on that."

Finally she stood on legs that threatened to give way, and retrieved her purse, her hands unsteady as she pulled out the two notes she'd tucked safely inside a pair of Ziploc plastic bags.

Griff blew out his breath in a sigh of relief as he rose and stepped over next to her. His hand brushed her shoulder in silent reassurance.

By the time he laid the bags on the table to study them, his pulse was already hammering.

"Torn from a cheap spiral notebook, just like the blank sheets on the other cars," he muttered. "Block printing. Hard to analyze."

The first note was crinkled and stained, a testament to Sunny's attack, and the pencil marks were faint in places, but he could read it.

"You've messed with the wrong person this time Loveless. Tell the police anything about me and your kid will die."

He looked up. "He knows your name." So it *was* about revenge. A sliver of worry embedded itself under his skin. He'd hoped he was wrong.

"Where was this?"

"He stuffed it into my mouth, when he was on top of me. He whispered *Chew on this, Loveless.*"

"The leather gloves." He pictured her struggling, injured, lying on the asphalt in the rain, while the attacker held her down, wadded up the note and pushed it between her teeth.

She nodded, her tension palpable, her green

eyes burning his skin. She'd been through more than he'd imagined. As irritated as he'd been by her stubborn attempts to handle this herself, he had to admire her bravery.

He'd asked her to trust him, and she had finally agreed. He'd made her a promise. Now he had to live up to it. The hollow ache in his chest flared.

He scanned the second note as she sat back down across from him.

You're spending too much time with the police. Someone you know will be hurt.

Someone already had. He raised his gaze.

"What is it?" Sunny frowned, two tiny lines appearing between her eyebrows. She glanced down at the second note, and gasped. "Something's happened. That's why you came here."

Her voice rose in volume and pitch. She stood so abruptly that the kitchen chair nearly tipped over.

"Ms. Loveless—"

"What's happened? It's not Emily, is it?" She covered her mouth, her eyes widening until white showed all the way around her emerald-colored irises. "Please—tell me she's okay."

"It's not Emily," he said, rounding the table and wrapping her ice-cold fingers in his, to warm them, he told himself. "But it is connected to one of your cases."

She took a long, shaky breath. "One of my cases?"

He nodded grimly. "Come sit down. Are you okay?"

She nodded jerkily.

He watched her, listened to her breathing. He held her chair for her, then sat next to her.

"Joseph Mabry is dead. He apparently fell down the stairs at his rooming house last night. One of his tenants found him around midnight."

"Mabry? The landlord from Jennifer Curry's case?" Her head jerked. "Was he…?"

Frustration burned inside Griff. He'd been at the scene all night, dogging CSU, but nothing concrete had turned up. "The M.E. has made a preliminary ruling of accidental death."

Sunny's wide eyes searched his face. "You don't believe it was an accident."

He shook his head. "Your baby disappears on Tuesday and a man connected with one of your cases dies under questionable circumstances on Thursday? I don't believe in coincidence. Tell me about Jennifer Curry."

"Two months ago she came to me, wanting to find her biological parents. Her adoptive mother had died. Jennifer found her adoption papers and a note in her mother's things. The documents weren't legal, and the note said 'Jane called. $20,000 by Friday.' It looked like Jennifer's mother had bought her from 'Jane.'"

Her voice was bitter, reminding Griff of her own history. Jennifer's case had been personal for her.

"The hospital and court records I was able to access didn't tell me anything. I figured Jane had needed help with those forged documents, so I checked out Vanderbilt University. There were seven Janes listed in the school's directory for 1989. Nine for 1990. I tried to find them all. But only one was the wife of a law student. Ed and Jane Gross lived at Mabry's place until 1991."

1991. Griff's tried to ignore the sudden burning ache in his chest and concentrated on the information Sunny had just given him. "So what did you find out from Mabry?"

"Not much. He remembered them. Couldn't swear Jane Gross had ever been pregnant. There's no proof the Grosses are Jennifer's parents."

"But you think they are?"

She nodded. "I think so. You think the Grosses killed Mabry?"

"Yes, I do. Because of something Mabry told you."

"But he didn't tell me anything. Just that they'd

lived there, and then one night they disappeared. I even flew to New York to talk to Ed Gross. He claimed he and his wife had never had a child. I let it drop and gave Jennifer her money back."

Griff frowned. "Do you always give up so easily?"

She stiffened. "I draw the line at invading people's privacy. I believe Ed Gross is Jennifer's father, but he obviously doesn't want to acknowledge it. He has that right."

"Did you tell Jennifer?"

"No. That would be unethical, and it would hurt her unnecessarily. I told her I had contacted the most likely candidate, but that it was a dead end."

"How did she take that?"

"Not well. She's a very angry young woman. Her mother had never told her she was adopted." She paused. "You think *Jennifer* did this? She's only eighteen—a child!"

"An adult. And you just told me she's angry."

"Why would she kill Mabry? If she's angry at anyone, it's me."

"Or the Grosses. When you met with Ed Gross, did he threaten you? Did he say anything suspicious?"

"No. He just snapped at me that he and his wife didn't have any children. He was lying."

"Yeah? How can you be so sure?"

Her mouth turned up in a tiny smile. "He was a terrible liar. He started sweating as soon as I told him why I was there. He couldn't wait to be rid of me."

"Well, someone thinks Mabry told you something. Something they didn't want to go any further."

Sunny stared at him with those wide green eyes that demanded loyalty and truth.

He didn't have a shred of proof, but he knew in his gut that Mabry's death had been no accident. "That means, Ms. Loveless, that not only is your baby in danger, so are you."

She laughed, a choked, desperate sound. "You think I care about me? I don't! All I care about is Emily."

"I understand." He did. All too well.

"Tell me the truth. Do you think Emily is okay? They'd need to keep her safe, right? To be sure I cooperate?"

He heard in her voice that she didn't believe her own words. Reluctantly, he met her gaze. "I wish I could—"

"Just tell me."

Griff spoke as calmly as he could. "I'm sorry, Ms. Loveless. We have no way of knowing if she's still alive or not. I know how hard this is—"

Sunny's anguished gaze met his, and a flame of fury glinted in her green eyes. "Do you have children, Agent Stone?" she asked coldly.

He winced. "No."

She lifted her chin as a single tear rolled down her cheek. "Then you cannot possibly know how hard this is."

Chapter Four

Griff felt as if she'd slapped him.

During his years with the FBI, he'd heard those
words before. And each time he heard them, they
tore another hole in his heart.

He'd consoled frantic parents whose desperate
fear turned into rage against the people who were
trying to help them, because they couldn't get to
the kidnappers. So he'd always responded with
respect, concern and assurance. Usually his calm
demeanor consoled the terrified families.

He'd never taken it personally. His feelings
didn't matter. He was a professional. His job was
not to share his private anguish, it was to offer
comfort and find the truth. He'd never even been
tempted to share his own personal feelings.

Until now.

He clenched his jaw against the urge to tell
Sunny that he did know exactly how hard it was
for her, that he'd been through it all himself. It

would do her no good to know that he spent a part of every single day searching for his sister.

"I apologize, Ms. Loveless," he said. "You're right."

Sunny looked at him curiously, her hands squeezed so tightly together that her knuckles were stark white.

"Some of the very best agents the FBI has are working on your little girl's case right now. What I need from you is a promise to cooperate fully. The more we know, the better our chances. You can't do this alone."

Sunny nodded, her head bent. "I know that." She lifted her head, her face taut with pain. "I hope I haven't waited too long.

Her lower lip trembled. A tear gathered at the corner of her eye and slipped down her cheek.

He knew she was terrified of what the kidnapper might do.

So was he.

He read through the second note again.

Remember, I'm watching you.

"Have you noticed anyone following you? Any cars sitting outside?"

"People park on the street. I haven't noticed any strange vehicles, but I've had other things on my mind. You should ask Lil."

"I will." He gestured. "You're sure you don't have any idea what the kidnapper is hiding?"

"I'm sure. I've never had an unhappy client."

"Never? What about Jennifer? I'm sure there are others you haven't been able to help."

"Well, yes, but I've given each of them a full refund. I wouldn't classify them as unhappy."

"It doesn't have to be an unhappy client. For instance, what was your most recent case?" Griff knew about all her cases, but he wanted her to talk about them. She'd been there, seen things that wouldn't be found in a case file.

She sniffed impatiently. "A couple of weeks ago an elderly lady hired me to contact the members of her high school cheerleading squad. It was very simple. I found most of them via the Internet. The rest I located through friends and alumni records from the high school. She's planning a reunion now." She shook her head. "I don't understand. The people I help have nothing against me. Why would they steal my daughter?"

"What if one of those cheerleaders had just poisoned her son-in-law because he'd been beating his wife, her daughter?"

"Are you kidding me?" Sunny laughed in disbelief.

Griff spread his hands. "Not the greatest

example in the world, but in working on a case, you could innocently stumble upon a crime in progress, or someone like Gross, who's running for office and doesn't want his dirty laundry aired. Your questions could push an unstable person over the edge."

Sunny's eyes narrowed.

Good. Griff felt a surge of triumph. She was getting over the idea of her clients as innocent people she was bound to protect.

"You need to change the way you think about your cases. Forget the *happy endings* cr—stuff. Think of each client as a suspect, guilty until proven innocent."

Her brow furrowed and her eyes snapped with irritation. "That defeats the whole purpose of my—"

"Tell me about every case you've ever had, no matter how small, starting with the cheerleaders. Were any of the ladies reluctant—" Griff stopped when his cell phone rang. He glanced at the Caller ID. It was Lieutenant Carver.

"Carver, what have you got?"

"Looks like Mabry's death is going to be ruled accidental."

Griff balled his fist. "Damn it. I need to see the CSI report and the medical examiner's findings."

"I'll arrange it. Meanwhile, I do have some

good news. Brittany Elliott came through with some information. Turns out that when her boyfriend got out of prison about two months ago, he contacted her. Told her he wanted her to go out West with him. Just her and their baby. He apparently became violent when he found out the same private investigator who'd gotten him sent to prison had adopted his child."

"Violent? Against the girl?"

"Nah. Busted up some furniture, though."

"Have you located him?"

"Not yet. We're still working on it."

"Okay, thanks. When you find him I want to talk to him." Griff paused. "Carver, I need a twenty-four hour watch on Ms. Loveless's house."

"I'm already devoting twelve man-hours a day to her, in case the kidnapper tries to contact her personally."

"The note on her windshield was a note from the kidnapper. It warned that someone she knows could be hurt."

"Was there a ransom demand?" Carver's voice rose in excitement.

"Nope. I believe the kidnapper is referring to Mabry's death, but just in case, I'd like an unmarked car in the area at all times."

"Can't do it. I'll make sure a black-and-white drives by every hour."

"Remove your officer from the house and give us a car instead. I don't think there's going to be a ransom demand. This isn't about money."

"I'll do what I can."

Griff disconnected.

He looked up to find Sunny staring intently at him.

"Who is Lieutenant Carver looking for?"

"Burt Means."

"I testified at his trial for statutory rape. Brittany was just fifteen. He was twenty."

Griff's gaze pinned her. "Well he's contacted her."

Her eyes widened in shock. "Has Lieutenant Carver found him?"

"No. They're still looking. Carver's contacting his parole officer."

"We've received some odd phone calls. Usually at night. We'll have to look in Lil's logbook, but I think one caller said something about meddling in other people's affairs. You think he could have done this?"

"It's a lead. Like I said earlier, most child abductions are perpetrated by a family member."

"But what about the Grosses?"

"They'll be questioned, of course. I don't believe Mabry's fall was an accident, but there's no evidence to link it to your case. I can't afford to ignore any possible lead. And neither can you."

"I understand that. I gave the list of odd phone calls to the police. We've always gotten crank calls, because of the 'happy endings' *stuff*. I've never worried much about them."

"Maybe you should have."

A flash of pain crossed her face. "It's easy for you to walk in here with your twenty-twenty hindsight."

She pulled the band out of her hair and combed her fingers through it. "Do you think I haven't lain awake at night, thinking about everyone I've come in contact with? Every case I've handled? Don't you think Lil and I have gone over every telephone call?"

Something in Griff's gaze shifted. The odd glints of blue and violet intensified. "I know you have." He reached out and stopped her nervous hand with his. "Tell me about them."

He put her hand on the table and patted it, then withdrew, but Sunny felt his taut resolve and reassurance. She didn't know why her case was so important to him. Maybe he approached every case with this single-minded intensity.

Even as the thought emerged, she knew it wasn't entirely true. He tried to maintain a businesslike demeanor. She understood that. She did the same thing. Remaining calm and detached while being sympathetic worked very well with nervous or distraught clients.

He'd started out that way with her, but underneath his professional exterior was a fervor that called to her.

Griff Stone was on a personal mission. She didn't know his reasons, but she understood that much. She'd been on one all her life. The sign on her door wasn't just a catchy logo. It was her goal. To find a happy ending for everyone. Including herself.

"Sunny? The phone calls?"

"Lil records all of them in a log. She also transcribes all the voice messages." Sunny smiled. "She was an IRS investigator. To her, everyone is suspicious."

Griff's mouth turned up. "Not a bad way to be. A little cynical, but healthy. So I take it you're not quite as conscientious?"

Sunny shook her head. "I'll get the book."

Griff followed her into the foyer that served as a reception area. "How did the burglar miss the telephone log?"

"About once a month, Lil takes it home with her to log our time. She had it that night."

Griff looked at the neat precise records. "These entries in purple are answering service messages?

"Right." She turned a few pages. "Here it is. March twenty-fifth. Lil has it recorded at eight-thirty p.m. She was keeping Emily. I was out of town overnight, working on a case."

Griff read the entry.

"Male voice. Age hard to tell. Possibly a phone booth. Background noise. 'You're messin' in people's lives. It's gonna get you in trouble.'"

He raised his eyebrows. "She wrote it in dialect?"

"Lil believes the way people talk can tell a lot about them. She spells the words the way she hears them, in case we need proof for an ID. She also downloads all the calls and voice messages onto CD."

"Where are the CDs?"

Sunny shook her head. "They were stolen in the break-in. Do you think the message was from Burt?"

"The timing is right. He would have just been released. But the warning is vague, nonspecific."

"Like the notes."

He nodded.

"What do you know about Means?"

"He apparently worked construction with

Brittany's best friend's older brother. Brittany's mother thought she was too young to date. So when she met Burt, she fell head over heels in love. You know how girls love the dangerous, physical type. Especially if they're off-limits."

He couldn't help but wonder what her tiny shrug meant. Nor could he stop himself from imagining what type she liked. Probably the safe, buttoned-down accountant type.

Although this morning, dressed in those light blue capri pants and a dark blue linen shirt over a little white tank top, with her hair down and no makeup on, she looked nothing like the stiff businesswoman he'd met yesterday.

Griff's cell phone rang. "Yeah?"

Sunny turned pages in the logbook, looking for other odd entries.

Griff muttered a curse and closed his phone. "That was Carver again. Means's parole officer came up empty on his whereabouts. He hasn't been in touch with him for over a week now. And he's been in contact with Brittany Elliott again."

Sunny's heart thumped in her throat. "You think he has Emily? What did Brittany say?"

Was Emily in the hands of her angry biological father, who probably felt that he'd been wrongly imprisoned, and blamed Sunny for his troubles?

"Brittany's mother heard her on the phone. But Brittany swears she hasn't seen him since he got out."

"They need to check her phone records—home and cell, and put somebody on her to watch her movements."

Griff's eyes sparked with a touch of disguised amusement.

She bit her lip. "They already are."

He nodded, and let his hand brush her shoulder, nothing more than a touch, but the gesture comforted her. "You're not the investigator in this case. You're the mother. Let the police do their job, and you do yours. Show me the other odd messages, and try to remember any threats you've received, no matter how innocuous they seemed."

Sunny continued going through the telephone log book with Griff watching over her shoulder.

The front doorbell rang. She looked up as the police officer on duty answered it.

It was Fred, the mailman.

"Hi, Sunny," Fred said, peering around the bulky form of the officer. "Got something for you." He held it up and wiggled it. "Funny thing, though, it doesn't have a stamp—"

"Hold it!" the officer barked. "Put that down."

Sunny's heart jumped into her throat. "What's the matter?" She stood and rounded the desk.

"Stand back, ma'am," the officer cautioned, as Griff pushed past her.

Fred froze, wide-eyed. "It looked harmless enough. I thought maybe—"

"Put it down." Griff commanded. "Carefully."

Fred, pale and shaky, set the package on the ground and backed away from it.

Griff crouched down beside the package and studied the writing and wrapping.

"The print is block letters." He pulled out his cell phone and dialed Carver.

"Carver, get the bomb squad over here. We've got a suspicious package. Small, about six by four inches. Height maybe three inches." He snapped his phone shut and rose. "Officer, take the mailman outside and get a statement."

The officer nodded and gestured to Fred, who followed him willingly.

"Sun—Ms. Loveless, go outside. Did I understand that Lillian lives next door?"

"Yes."

"Get her and go down the block. At least two more houses. Wait there."

"What are you going to do?" Sunny asked, eyeing the package.

"Stay here with the package."

"No!" Sunny surprised herself by the vehemence of her outburst.

Griff looked up at her.

"I mean—if it's a bomb, you should get away from it, too."

He shook his head. "Someone has to guard it."

"Well, why does it have to be you? Can't we watch it from across the street or something?"

"I'll watch it. You go with Lillian."

"I'm staying with you."

"That's an unnecessary risk. What good are you going to be to Emily if you get yourself blown to bits? Get out of here."

Chastened, Sunny had to admit that he was right. Reluctantly, she stepped over to the door. "At least stand outside until the bomb squad gets here, please? You're not going to be any good to—to me if you get blown up."

Griff sighed and rose.

Sunny's limbs went limp with relief. She did not want this man's blood on her conscience. It was suddenly terribly important to her that he stay healthy and whole.

It was probably because he seemed to know what she was going through. He seemed to care about finding Emily as much as she did. But as he'd stood, and his thigh muscles rippled under the crisp khaki of his pants, she'd been surprised by the tiny thrill that slid through her. How wonderful it would be to have a man like Griff to care for her, to hold her during the scary times, to share the good times.

Reluctantly, she turned her back and left the house, listening to be sure he followed her.

When the bomb squad got there, one lanky, buzz-cut guy immediately took charge of the scene, dispatching uniformed officers to knock on doors up and down the street.

Lillian answered her door. Immediately she pointed toward Sunny and said something to the officer, who shook his head, and led her down the street, away from Sunny's house.

Sunny waved reassuringly at her.

"Go on," Griff said. "Go with Lillian."

"I want to stay here."

"That's not a good idea."

Sunny glanced up at him. "I'll go when you go."

Griff scowled at her.

The buzz-cut guy was still barking orders and gesturing. All at once her attention zeroed in on his hand. He was missing two fingers. Memories of that awful night washed over her.

She'd almost forgotten the distinguishing feature she'd noticed on her attacker. Through the leather gloves, she'd had the impression that her attacker was missing a finger—maybe two.

She couldn't pinpoint when or how she'd come

to that conclusion—something about the way the leather had flopped against her chin as the note had been stuffed into her mouth.

She resolved to tell Griff as soon as she had a chance.

From her vantage point next to Griff, Sunny watched two men suit up in protective gear and carry a device from their truck, down the sidewalk and up the front steps to her door.

"That's an X-ray machine," Griff said. He stood beside her, his arms crossed, his foot tapping. He obviously wanted to be in the middle of the action.

"Have you seen many bombs?" she asked.

"A few."

"Are you going to feel silly if it's the box of business cards I ordered?"

"No. And it's not."

"It's the right size."

He cut his eyes over to her. "Too light."

She nodded, swallowing nervously, as the two men who'd delivered the X-ray machine to her front door retreated, leaving the officer in charge alone in her house with a potential bomb.

She hugged herself, cringing, expecting an explosion any second.

A voice distorted by static crackled over a mobile telecom unit. She couldn't make out what it said, but one of the suited-up men jogged up the street from the police van to her house and went in. Through the door, she could see him and another man crouched near the package.

They seemed to confer for a long time. Then the officer in charge took something from his pocket.

"He's going to open it," Griff said softly. He took her arm and gently led her farther down the street, toward the bomb squad's van that was parked about sixty yards from her house. "You should always be at least as far away as the bomb squad members. They know what a safe distance is."

Sunny looked back over her shoulder at her front door, seeing the forms disappear as she and Griff moved farther away.

A sudden shout startled her and she grasped Griff's hand.

"That was a warning to clear the area around the house."

Her shoulders tensed and she leaned in toward Griff. His arm slipped lightly around her shoulders. The air reverberated with tense silence.

Then she heard a muffled pop.

The officers in the van didn't move.

After what seemed like a very long time, a silhouette appeared in Sunny's doorway. He took off his helmet and yelled, "All clear."

Sunny's breath whooshed out in a huge sigh. "Wh-what was that pop?"

One of the bomb squad members heard her. "A blasting cap, ma'am."

"Agent Stone." It was the officer in charge.

Griff let go of Sunny's shoulder and headed toward the house. Sunny followed.

The officer took her in at a glance as he began talking to Griff.

"Blasting cap. We identified wires and the cap on the X-ray, but couldn't tell what else might be in there."

"What about the characteristics?"

He shrugged. "Crude. Simple. Almost anyone could do it, following instructions on the Internet or in books. It's easy to put together. The problem for amateurs comes when they try to put explosives in it. That's a lot trickier. Plus it's a little more difficult to obtain C-4 or other explosives than it is to get blasting caps."

Sunny listened, confused. "But if it was just a blasting cap and some wires, then what was he trying to do?"

Griff looked at her. "Scare you. Warn me." He turned back to the officer in charge. "Can we have the package now?"

The officer nodded. "Sure. It's all yours."

"Get me a paper bag," Griff said to Sunny.

She stepped around the package and retrieved a grocery bag from the kitchen.

Griff had pulled on latex gloves by the time she got back. He carefully lifted the opened package and placed it in the bag just as Carver approached.

"That your bomb?" Carver asked.

Griff stood and handed him the bag and the notes Sunny had given him. "Make sure CSU goes over all this with a fine-tooth comb. Check the printing on this and the two notes—see if they match."

Carver's eyebrows flew upward when he saw the notes, and he shot Sunny a look of irritation. "*Two* notes?"

She lowered her gaze.

"I'll get CSU on it," he said to Griff. "We'll see if we can lift any prints, too. What was the bomb?"

"Crude. Blasting cap triggered to go off when the package was opened."

"Mmm, could have cost a finger or two." Carver frowned. "Who do you think—Means?"

"It's worth checking out. Working in construction, he might have access to blasting caps. I'll write up the report on the notes and get it to you."

Even after the officers and the bomb squad van left, Sunny couldn't stop trembling. She wouldn't have given a thought to opening a package. She or Lil could have been injured.

"I don't understand," she said to Griff. "Who would send me a fake bomb? Why? What were they trying to accomplish?"

"I told you, it could have been a warning, a scare tactic, a diversion. It might not even be connected to the kidnapping."

"Not connected?"

"Emily's disappearance has gotten a lot of publicity. In addition to the Grosses and Emily's biological father, there are others who aren't happy with you—Thomas the deadbeat dad, Jennifer Curry. I have copies of your case files from the police. There's almost always an injured party—even if it's only in their own mind."

With every word Griff spoke, Sunny felt her carefully constructed fantasy crumbling. "I don't understand. All I ever wanted to do was help people. Give them the happy ending they were looking for."

Griff just looked at her, his face carefully blank. "Haven't you figured it out yet? There are no happy endings."

GRIFF RAPPED on the open door of Lieutenant Carver's office. The older man was on the phone, but he waved Griff in.

"No, you stay on the canvassing. I'll go over and talk to her parents." Carver wiped his face. "Thanks."

When Carver hung up, Griff stepped closer to his desk and handed him three sheets of paper. "Here's the report I promised you about the notes Sun—Ms. Loveless received."

"Great. Nice of her to finally tell us about 'em."

"She was afraid. They told her they'd kill her baby."

Carver's bushy brows drew down as he angled a glance at Griff. "They all say that."

Griff nodded, chagrined. He sounded like a rookie. Worse, he sounded like a rookie with a crush on a crime victim, and he knew that was exactly what the veteran police lieutenant was thinking.

Carver heaved a big sigh and nodded toward a chair. "Sit down. I've got news."

Griff didn't like the tone of Carver's voice. This didn't sound good. He sat. "Is it about Mabry?"

"First of all, the preliminary report on the notes is that the first one was written by a different person than note number two or the lettering on the fake bomb."

"Yeah?"

Carver nodded. "Our handwriting expert states

that the second note and the address on the package could be the same person."

Griff filed that information away. "What else?"

"Brittany Elliott's missing."

Griff's pulse sped up. "She's gone to her boyfriend, Means."

Carver nodded.

"What do the parents say? When did she disappear?"

"Apparently she was supposed to spend the night with her best friend. When she didn't come home by noon, her parents called the friend's parents. Brittany hadn't been there."

"Damn. I didn't expect this. Means's profile doesn't fit with stealing the baby. Not unless it was for money."

"Doesn't fit? Why not? He's the baby's father."

"Our profiler has studied his history. He's from an abusive family. Ran away from home, never finished high school. He's emotionally immature. Fatherhood would be way too much responsibility. Now if the girl had been with him from the beginning, it would make more sense. She might have coaxed him into getting her baby back for her."

"We're still searching for them. We can't rule them out."

"I agree. I want to talk to Means soon as you

find him. And I don't care how long it's been, I want his hands tested for residue. I want to know if he set that blasting cap."

"I got the report from CSU. Inconclusive. It's a common brand, used all around this area. We're checking retailers, but I doubt that's gonna give us anything." Carver leaned back in his chair and sighed. "And there were no prints or trace evidence."

"What about the rigging?"

"Like the bomb squad leader said, it's a simple rig. Anyone who's ever worked construction, or can follow directions, can rig a cap to pop. According to the lab, it wasn't meant to be anything more than a scare tactic. Chances of injury were low, especially with such a small box."

Small box. "Wait a minute." Griff's pulse sped up. "The box was small enough to fit into the mailbox, so why did the mailman bring it to the door? He told Sunny it didn't have a stamp."

Carver shuffled papers on his desk. "The officer on duty at Ms. Loveless's house took his statement. Let me see." He reached for a file. "Here it is."

He read for a few seconds, then handed the typed report to Griff.

Griff scanned it. "He found the box in the mailbox and brought it to the house to let Ms.

Loveless know it didn't come through the regular mail." He looked up at Carver. "Could have been any time since the mail ran yesterday. Is someone canvassing the neighbors, to see if anyone saw anything?"

Carver nodded. "The street is pretty deserted during the day. Most of the residents work."

"So nobody saw **anything**." Griff stood. "I'm going to the M.E.'s office. See what they've found about Mabry's death." He paused at the Lieutenant's door. "Thanks. I know this is straining your resources."

Carver shrugged. "A baby's missing. Nobody's complaining about the work."

Griff nodded. These were good people, doing a good job. Whoever they were up against was either extraordinarily good or extraordinarily lucky.

HIRAM TURNED DOWN the volume on the police scanner and picked up his phone, nearly giddy with relief and excitement.

He punched in a number.

"What?" Janie's irritating screech hurt his ears, but right now he didn't care.

"Are you still watching the national news? 'Cause there's been a new development."

"I told you not to call me."

Anger caused sweat to pop out on his forehead. "Listen, you—" he stopped before he said the word he was thinking. It would be better not to cross Janie. He took a deep breath instead.

"Sunny Loveless received an explosive device in the mail today. They had to call in the bomb squad."

He couldn't help grinning. "According to the police scanners, they're looking for the baby's biological father and mother. The father is wanted for questioning, because he's worked in construction."

"Hmmph. If I want to talk to you, I'll call you." The line went dead.

Hiram looked at the phone, then threw it across the room. It bounced harmlessly against the wall and plopped onto the floor.

The twerp in the next apartment kicked the connecting wall and shouted, "Keep it down in there!"

Hiram muttered an appropriate response under his breath. The guy worked nights, and he got mean if woken up during the day.

Moving to the table, Hiram turned up the volume on the scanner as high as he dared. If anything else happened to Sunny Loveless, he wanted to hear about it.

Chapter Five

73 hours missing

It was after nine o'clock when Sunny waved good-night to Lillian, and watched as her friend crossed the yard to her own house. As soon as Lillian was safely inside her house, Sunny closed and locked the front door. She turned out the lights in the foyer and wearily climbed the stairs.

The excitement over the fake bomb had finally died down, and Sunny had spent a grueling couple of hours being questioned by Agent Stone—Griff. He'd grilled her about every single case she'd had in the two years her agency had been in business.

He was kind, but relentless. And he was good. He'd coaxed tidbits of information from her memory that she hadn't known she knew.

Like the glint of venom in Bob Thomas's eye. She'd forgotten how the man had looked at her that day in court, right after he'd been harangued by the judge for not paying child support.

Or the hostility in the young woman's voice when Sunny had contacted her to tell her that her brother wanted to end a ten-year estrangement between them. The woman had coldly told Sunny that some things could never be forgiven. At the time, Sunny had sympathized with the brother, who'd seemed brokenhearted that his sister didn't want to see him. But today, Griff's intense gaze made her wonder if she'd done the right thing.

When Griff asked her if she'd given the man any hint of where his sister was, Sunny's heart had hammered in trepidation. Had she? What if the brother was violent or abusive? Had she put the woman in danger? The man had sat in Sunny's office, with her case notes in plain view on her desk.

Griff's scowl told her what he was too polite to say. He thought she was careless and incompetent. *Fluff*.

Right now, she agreed with him. She'd had an idealistic notion of helping people by giving them the happy ending they sought. It warmed her heart each time she helped reunite friends, or bring together long-lost family members.

But Griff had forced her to see how naive she'd been. The harsh truth had been reflected in his violet eyes.

Every one of her cases had its dark side, its un-answered questions. Almost any one of them could have spawned a bitter person who resented her intrusion.

At the top of the stairs, she wrapped her arms around her stomach and hugged herself. She felt beaten down. Sick with worry.

For the first time in six months, since Emily had come into her life, the weight of her loneliness en-shrouded her. It was amazing how thoroughly one tiny little being had taken over her heart. The gaping hole left when her parents had died had been filled to overflowing by her beautiful little girl.

A small moan escaped her lips as she stopped at the door to Emily's room. She filled her lungs with the sweet, baby powder smell of her daughter. And felt the emptiness return.

The moonlight turned the bright pink-and-yel-low room to a soft, muted beige. The baby bed sat by the window, its little blankets unwrinkled, its baby pillow smooth and undented by Emily's tiny head.

As tears began to flow down her cheeks, Sunny tiptoed over and picked up the stuffed bear she'd had made especially for her daughter. She sat in the rocking chair, hugging the bear to her chest.

"Oh, Emily," she choked. Was she ever going

to see her sweet baby girl again? The fear that had dogged her all her life, the reason she had formed Loveless, Inc. two years ago, echoed in her ears in Griff's low deep voice.

There are no happy endings.

She pushed her nose into the bear's soft fur. "Dear God, please. I will do anything. Just don't let them hurt her. I promised her I'd take care of her. Help me keep that promise. Please don't take her away from me."

Old grief mixed with new, tasting like ashes in her mouth. Without Emily to fill the void in her soul, Sunny missed her mom and dad with a fierceness that surprised her. Her parents had been in their fifties when her mother had found her, a newborn, abandoned in the parking lot of the hospital where she'd worked the evening shift. The Lovelesses had immediately started proceedings to adopt her. As far as Sunny was concerned, they were her family.

Just as she was Emily's family. Her throat clogged with tears and she rocked back and forth, her chest cramping with a pain too deep for tears.

She finally understood what her mother had always told her. *You could not be more special. Not even if I'd carried you inside me.*

A harsh jangle startled her. It was her cell phone.

Her heart skipped with hope and fear. In the three days since her baby had been stolen, her cell phone hadn't rung once.

Only Lillian and a few close friends had the number. She'd given it to Lieutenant Carver so he could reach her no matter where she was.

But the number was engraved on the gold ID bracelet Lil had given Emily just a week before, for her six-month birthday.

She dug the phone out of her pocket and flipped it open. She didn't recognize the number. Her hand shook so much that she almost dropped the phone.

"Hello?" she said cautiously, afraid to hope, afraid to think this was anything other than a wrong number.

"Ms. Loveless?"

The voice was gruff but definitely female. And tense.

Sunny's heart thudded in her chest. The bear fell from her lap as she cupped both hands around the tiny phone.

Was this the call? The ransom request?

"Y-yes?" She clenched her jaw to keep from screaming *Where is my baby?*

"You don't know me," the woman said nervously, her voice almost drowned out by the sound of traffic in the background. "But—"

"Do you have my baby?" Sunny croaked.

"Emily is right here. She's just fine."

Sunny's breath caught between a sob and a gasp. "Oh, thank God." Her scalp tightened as the edge of her vision went dark and her knees gave way. She crumpled to the floor, huddled over the phone.

"Please, please, tell me where she is. Give my baby back to me. I'll do anything." Sobs racked her body.

"Ms. Loveless, listen to me. I can't stay on the phone. You have to come to Philadelphia, alone."

Sunny tried to concentrate on the woman's words. "Phila-Philadelphia? Pennsylvania?" What was she talking about? "Is that where you are? Where Emily is?"

"Ms. Loveless, I need to know that I can trust you not to tell anyone. Not the police. Not the FBI. Not even your family. It's a matter of life or death."

"Oh, God!" Fear slashed her heart. "Please, no. Don't hurt her. I'll do whatever you want. I don't have much money, but—"

"Oh, no, ma'am." The woman sounded horrified. "I'm not asking for money. But the people who took your baby are very dangerous. I don't know what they'll do if they find out I've contacted you. They're capable of anything. Do you understand?"

"The people who—? No, I don't understand. Don't *you* have her?" Sunny clutched her stomach as bile clawed at her throat.

"I do, ma'am. I do. For now. She's safe and warm and happy."

A moan escaped Sunny's numb lips. "What do you want from me?"

"I just want all this to stop. You deserve to have your baby back, safe and sound. But you have to come alone, and you have to come now! They'll be back any day now."

"Who are they? And who are you?"

"I can't tell you that. When you get to Philadelphia, call this number." She rattled off ten digits.

Sunny stood on shaky legs. "Wait. I have to find a pen."

"I can't. I've got to go."

Sunny repeated the numbers, doing her best to commit them to memory.

"Come as soon as you can. If you don't hurry, it will be too late."

Too late. Oh please God no. "Where in Philadelphia? Where do I go?"

"Just call the number." The line went dead.

Sunny ran into her bedroom and grabbed a pen and paper from her desk. She wrote the number down, praying that she hadn't transposed any of the digits.

Then she sank into her desk chair, her limbs quivering, her stomach churning. She looked at her phone, and hit star 69. But the phone on the other end just rang and rang.

Dropping the cell phone onto her desk, Sunny squeezed her head between her hands as dry, panicked sobs shook her.

Philadelphia. Emily was in Philadelphia.

She had to go. Alone. She couldn't tell anyone about the phone call. The woman had said the people who'd taken Emily were dangerous. *Capable of anything.* There was no time to waste.

Her baby's life was at stake.

BESS HUNG UP the pay phone and hurried back to her pickup.

She climbed into the front seat and leaned over to check on Emily. Talking to the baby's mother had upset her more than she'd realized.

"Hey, Emily Rose. You still asleep?"

The baby's pale lashes rested against her rosy cheeks. Bess's eyes filled with tears. "I just talked to your mommy," she whispered. "She's coming to get you. She'll be here soon, I promise."

As Bess straightened and turned the ignition key a cold sweat popped out on her forehead. Her left arm tingled. She reached for her purse and took out a tiny prescription bottle.

"One of these little tablets should—" She tried to take a full breath, but couldn't. "And I'll be fine. Let's go home. Old Bess is tired and it's a forty-minute drive back to the house."

A heaviness weighed on her, a sense of dread anticipation. She was scared to death that Janie would return for Emily before her mother got to Philadelphia. She had to do something.

"I'll tell you what, Emily. I'm really worried that Janie has gone round the bend this time." She felt a familiar flush as the heart medication took effect. "And I'm getting too old for this. You know what I'm going to do?" She smiled as Emily cooed in her sleep.

"That's right. I'm going to call Mia. She'll help me make sure you're safe. Out of Janie's reach."

SUNNY THREW HER PURSE and Emily's pink diaper bag into the passenger seat of her car.

She ducked her head and ran back toward the house as the rain intensified. All she needed was her suitcase.

Then, over the downpour, she heard the crunch of a footstep on gravel.

Just like the night Emily had been kidnapped.

Panic streaked through her. She jerked her head up. A bulky form loomed over her and a rough arm grabbed her.

"No!" she shrieked, kicking, elbowing—anything to stop the assault. "Help!"

"Shut up!" A hand that smelled of motor oil and cigarettes clamped over her mouth.

She clawed at it, tried to bite it, but he was too strong. He dragged her up the steps and through her front door. She struggled not to lose her footing.

He kicked the door shut and pushed her against the banister. "All right, Loveless! I warned you I'd pay you back."

She could barely see through her wet plastered hair, but the man's bulk and his voice were familiar. Dread filled her at the hatred that blasted her.

"Get off me! What do you want?"

"You know what I want!" The voice was harsh and furious.

Sunny wiped her face with trembling hands, and squinted at the bulky form in the light from the front porch. The short haircut, combined with the familiar voice, told her who he was.

Burt Means!

Her pulse hammered. The last thing he'd said to her was etched in her memory.

You'll pay for this, he'd mouthed at her as the guards had led him out of the courtroom.

"It's you! Where's my baby?" she managed to say as he grabbed her shoulders.

"*Your* baby?" he thundered, shaking her.

His hands were punishingly strong. Pain shot through her bones. She could barely think.

"Stop it!" She tried to kick him. "Get off me!"

"It's my kid! Don't mess with me! Where's my kid?"

Sunny went limp with horrified shock. "You don't have her?" Was he lying? Had she heard wrong? Confusion and dread turned her stomach.

"You hid her, didn't you?" he yelled. "When you heard I was getting out. You knew I'd come after her—*and* you!"

He shoved her away and lifted his hand as if to hit her.

Sunny cringed and recoiled.

"You ruined my life *and* took my kid. Well, you won't get away with it."

She held up her hands to ward off his blow. "Oh, my God, you really don't have her? You didn't have that woman call—?"

He paused. "What woman? Stop lying! I saw you put the diaper bag in your car."

"No! Please," she cried. "I swear I don't know where she is." Her chest cramped. She couldn't draw a full breath.

Burt didn't have her baby!

He shoved her toward the staircase. "Is she upstairs? You'd better start talking, and fast."

If Burt didn't have Emily…

Her breath hitched as fear and grief enveloped her. "She's not here. I thought you'd taken her— or Brittany had." She looked at the hulk who towered over her. "But you're not the one who attacked me. You're too big."

Burt wrenched her arm and stared at her for an instant, then his lip curled in a snarl. "You're a smart one, aren't you? Here's what we're going to do. We're going through every inch of this house, and if that kid's not here, you're going to take me to her."

"I can't—" Sunny cried out as Burt twisted her arm until her shoulder burned with pain.

"Well you better, 'cause if you don't…" His snarl turned into a leer. "Before we're done tonight I'll make you beg me to kill you."

GRIFF PUSHED AWAY from the hotel room's writing desk. He'd spent the past half hour studying his missing child database, looking for similarities between Sunny's case and others, the way he did each time he heard of another missing child. He wanted to scroll down to the bottom of the file and look at the first case entered there. But that case wasn't relevant to this one. He had a job to do, a missing child to find. This was no time for wallowing in grief and self-recrimination.

He rubbed his stubbled jaw. He was having trouble concentrating.

It had been a long day, starting at three o'clock this morning when Carver had called him about Mabry's suspicious death.

He paced deliberately in front of the glass wall that looked out over the Nashville skyline and tried to think about the M.E.'s report on Mabry's death. It didn't work. All he could see before his eyes was the hurt in Sunny's expression when he'd snapped at her.

There are no happy endings. It had been a cruel and thoughtless comment, born from his own pain—his own failure. He'd been focused inward on the grief that had consumed him ever since he got here.

Nashville. That was the problem. The city where he'd grown up was calling to him, reminding him, accusing him.

He stared out over the city's streets, laid out like the spokes of a wheel. They were fast turning shiny and reflective with the rain that had begun to fall.

Nashville had changed a lot since he'd been gone, yet the skyline remained familiar. He knew exactly where Centennial Park was. His gaze zeroed in on the lights that defined the downtown park with its replica of the ancient Parthenon.

Old grief settled deep in his belly. He turned away from the window, and his gaze landed on the screen of his laptop. The screen saver had come on.

Outside, the city taunted him with whispers of traffic and rain as he stared at the slide show of pictures from that fateful summer day when he'd taken his toddler sister to that very park.

If he hadn't been so interested in his new camera, if he hadn't turned his back on Marianne's stroller to snap a picture of a dog jumping to catch a Frisbee...

He muttered a curse, and took two giant strides over to the desk and shut off the computer.

If he hadn't...

But he had. That few seconds of distraction had given Marianne's abductor time to grab her and run.

He kept the photos on his screen saver, not to remind him of that day—he needed no help with that—but to keep his sister's face in his mind.

To keep her alive.

He slid his laptop into its case and locked it, mindful of the FBI case notes and files it contained. He took it everywhere. He even kept a change of clothes and a few sundries in the compact case.

Back at the window, he pulled the drapes. With

the city hidden behind yards of material, maybe he could get some sleep.

He looked at his watch. Ten o'clock. He was exhausted, but he was too antsy to rest. He couldn't sit, couldn't relax. He sure as hell had no hope of sleeping.

He wondered how Sunny was doing. It had been a long day for her, too. First, he'd shocked her with the information about Mabry's death.

Then there had been the fake bomb, which he still didn't understand. Even though Burt Means theoretically had access to blasting caps, the gratuitous display didn't seem to fit with the rest of the case. There was a chance it was coincidental, but he didn't think so. It seemed more like a diversionary tactic.

Whatever its purpose, it had certainly spooked Sunny. Then to top it all off, he'd slammed her in the face with his cruel remark about happy endings, then put her through the third degree, questioning her for hours about every case she'd ever handled.

She'd been pale and drawn by the time he'd left to check in with Carver about the package. Her friend Lillian had been there, eyeing him with her sharp, disapproving gaze. She thought he was being too hard on Sunny.

He was. But he had to make sure she didn't

hide any more information from him. And if he had to destroy her rosy dreams in order to save her child, he would.

Feeling a little dirty, he took a quick shower, telling himself it would make him feel drowsy. It didn't work. He couldn't get Sunny Loveless's hurt green eyes out of his mind.

He knew she was all right—she had Lillian to take care of her. But he'd feel better if he heard her say it. He didn't allow himself to consider any other motive as he took out his cell phone and dialed her home number.

No answer.

His first instinct was to rush over to her house, but he stopped and forced himself to think logically. Maybe Lillian had managed to get her to go to bed early.

He looked toward his own bed and sighed. It was no use. He'd never get to sleep until he'd checked on her.

He pulled on jeans, a T-shirt and a white dress shirt, stuck his gun in its paddle holster at the small of his back and shrugged into a lightweight sport coat.

Habit made him grab the computer case before he headed downstairs. Outside, the rain had increased, but it was a quick sprint to his rental car.

Once he was headed toward East Nashville, he felt a little silly. Sunny's house would be dark and still, and he had no reason to wake her.

He was just restless, and checking on her was nothing more than an excuse to assuage his guilt for his remark about no happy endings.

All he was going to do was drive down her street, then turn around and head back to the hotel and face a long sleepless night. He supposed he could stop in at one of the clubs where aspiring country stars sang their hearts out, hoping to be noticed by a record producer. But that held no interest for him. Not tonight.

He turned onto Kenyon Avenue, his windshield wipers slapping in rhythm with the blues guitar playing on the car's radio. The neighborhood was quiet and dark, blanketed by the rain. A few cars were parked on the street, but everyone seemed to be tucked in for the night.

However, as soon as Sunny's house came into view, he realized something was wrong. Her porch light was on and her front door was wide open.

What the hell? He killed his lights and pulled to the curb, his pulse racing. He jumped out and drew his gun. He had to blink to keep the rain out of his eyes as he crept toward two shadowy figures he could barely make out through the rain.

Two figures.

Sunny was in trouble.

Thankful for the curtain of rain that hid him, Griff quietly dialed 911, identified himself and requested immediate backup. Then he crept through Lillian's yard.

By the time he was close enough to hear anything over the roar of the rain, the bulky figure had opened the driver's side door of Sunny's car.

"Stop your blubbering and get in the damn car," a harsh voice said as meaty arms pushed a drenched and shaking Sunny into the driver's seat.

Feeling a powerful urge to coldcock the bully, Griff silently stepped up behind him and pressed the barrel of his gun to the back of his head. "Freeze, or I'll blow your head off."

The man froze for an instant, then jerked backward, but Griff was ready. He shoved the bigger man against the open car door and sank the barrel of his gun an inch into the back of his neck.

"I said freeze! Now, spread your legs and put your hands on your head. Make a move and your hands won't have anything to rest on." Griff heard the fury in his own voice.

Apparently the man did, too. He spewed invectives, but he stayed still.

Griff wanted to check on Sunny, but he didn't dare take his attention off his quarry until backup arrived. He pushed the gun barrel in another fraction of an inch.

The bully tensed. "Ow! Careful, man. That thing might go off."

Rage burned inside Griff. "Yeah, it might," he growled. "My Glock doesn't like cowards who manhandle women."

Within seconds sirens pierced the sound of the rain. Thank God, Carver had made good on his promise to keep a police car in the area.

As two officers handcuffed the man and led him away, the rain slowed to a drizzle.

Griff bent and looked inside the car at Sunny. She was soaked to the skin. Her eyes were bloodshot and rimmed with smudged makeup.

To his surprise, when he held out his hand, she grabbed it and vaulted up into his arms.

SUNNY HADN'T MEANT to lose control like that. But she'd been praying that Griff would show up and save her from Burt, and suddenly, there he was, appearing out of the rain like a knight on a white horse.

She'd been so scared, and Griff's body was powerful and warm and safe. The stench of cigarettes and motor oil was replaced by Griff's calming scent. He smelled of rain and soap and a faint hint of cinnamon.

"It's okay, Sunny. It's okay. He's gone."

His low voice tickled her ear as he held her tightly.

She yearned to mold herself to him, to accept the comfort his body offered.

He'd promised her he'd give his life to find her child. At this moment, she believed he could do anything. She pressed her face into the hollow of his neck, soaking up his strength.

He took a sharp breath, stiffened, then stepped backward.

She'd been leaning against him, so she almost stumbled, but he grasped her upper arms to steady her.

Pain shrieked through her sore muscles. She cried out.

He frowned and loosened his grip. "Let's get inside."

Even though the temperature was mild and summery, Sunny began to shiver. She let Griff lead her up the steps and into the house.

"Towels?"

She pointed at the door on the left side of the foyer. The downstairs guest room had its own bath. "I—I'll get them," she said through chattering teeth.

But Griff ignored her and disappeared through

the door, reappearing a moment later with a white fluffy towel. He scrubbed his face and hair, then approached her.

She held out a shaky hand.

Griff cursed under his breath. "That sorry scumbag." His voice was harsh as he reached out toward her, his fingers stopping a fraction of an inch away from her arm.

She winced involuntarily, then looked down. Large red ovals on her skin were beginning to turn a deep blue-black.

"He hurt you." His voice was soft, but fury blazed from his eyes. "Did he—"

She shook her head, and rubbed her sore arms.

"Who was it? Did you know him?"

"It was Burt Means." She shivered, reaching for the towel.

"You're going to have to wait until the police examine you. Here. I'll dry your face."

Sunny closed her eyes as he gently, carefully patted away a few drops of water from her eyes. She shivered when he brushed a lock of wet hair off her forehead.

"He came here to get Emily." Tears clogged her throat. "He doesn't have her."

"You're sure?"

She nodded. "He was too angry. He's convinced I've hidden her somewhere."

"Yeah? Why would he think that?"

Sunny pushed a lock of wet hair out of her eyes. *Because he'd seen her putting Emily's diaper bag in her car.*

She couldn't tell Griff that. He would know immediately what she was planning to do. He'd know the kidnapper had contacted her again.

Holding her breath to keep from sobbing, she reminded herself that as tempting as it was to trust him, she couldn't. She had to get rid of him and the police as soon as possible, so she could get on the road to Philadelphia, to her baby. She'd lost too much time already.

"He demanded I take him to Emily. I tried to explain that I have no idea where she is. That's when he—" a shudder racked her body "—he said if I didn't tell him, before he was finished with me I'd beg him to kill me."

Griff's face darkened ominously. His jaw clenched. Turning on his heel, he stalked over to the front window. "The officer in charge will be in here in a minute. He can take your statement."

She stared at his broad back. His sport jacket and jeans were soaked, and clung to his lean, muscled body. His back was rigid, as if he was barely holding himself in check.

She shivered and felt her breasts tighten. Looking down, she realized what her wet clothes revealed. Her nipples were clearly outlined through the thin material of her top.

Oh no. She had on white slacks and thin silk bikini underwear. Everything—everything was probably visible through the wet transparent material. Her face burned. "I'm going upstairs to change."

"No." Griff turned. His gaze raked her from head to foot, lingering at the apex of her thighs. He blinked, then met her eyes, new fire burning in his.

Incredibly, Sunny felt her body react. She was terrified, still aching from Burt's brutality, but Griff's violet gaze stirred her.

"I told you, the police have to check your clothes and—you for trace evidence." His throat moved as he swallowed.

Just as Sunny opened her mouth to ask if she could wait in the kitchen, a knock sounded on the door and the police were there.

It was almost an hour before the last officer left, taking her wet clothes with him. She'd promised the officer in charge she'd come down to the station in the morning to file a report.

By the time they left, her nerves were frayed to the breaking point. She surreptitiously glanced at the clock. *Midnight*.

She had to get rid of Griff and get out of here. Emily was waiting.

Just a little longer, she told herself. If she could stay calm just a little longer, Griff would leave, and she could get on the road to Philadelphia and her baby.

Watching him take charge of the scene, directing the officers, her heart had yearned for his strength. But if she showed up with a lawman, the woman who had Emily would panic and run, and Sunny would lose her baby forever.

As the last of the police cars pulled away and Griff walked back up the steps toward her, she blocked the doorway.

"Thank you," she said, putting on a mask of relief, as if the knowledge that Burt Means was locked up had calmed all her fears.

He didn't stop, didn't acknowledge her gratitude. He stalked right past her into the house. With no other choice but to be overrun, she scrambled out of his way.

Standing in her foyer, he pushed his wet hair back with both hands, and slung the water away.

"All right. The police are gone. I want to know what the hell is going on."

She stared at him. "What—what do you mean?"

He sent her a disgusted look. "You gave the officer a good story."

"A good story?" Fear skittered up her spine.

Griffin Stone was too perceptive. Sometimes he terrified her.

Griff scowled. "You lied to the officers. How did Means get inside? The door wasn't forced, and I know you didn't let him in."

"He—" She couldn't think. "I'd gone outside. I was getting something out of my car."

His gaze drilled through her bravado. He was the enemy, standing between her and her baby. If she thought he would help her, she'd beg him. But he couldn't, not with this. She had to rescue Emily alone.

"Something out of your car," he repeated derisively. "What?"

Sunny was too tired and too beaten down to spar with him. At this moment, she couldn't remember what she'd told the police.

"My—my suitcase. I needed to unpack."

"Unpack." His voice held a cold derision. His eyes were hard as amethysts.

"Yes." She raised her chin. "Like I told the officer, I'm a terrible procrastinator. That suitcase has been in the car for over a week, since—since a trip I took." Her attempt at lying was a miserable failure. But she was desperate. She had to get rid of him and get on the road. Every minute wasted was a minute closer to *too late*.

His eyes accused her. "Right. Your suitcase, your

purse, your baby's diaper bag. I listened to your statement."

She nodded, her heart pounding so loud she was sure he could hear it.

He emitted a soft, sharp laugh and shook his head. "You're a really bad liar, Ms. Loveless."

"I'm not lying." Sunny clenched her teeth. "Now if you don't mind, I'm tired."

He started toward her. She stepped aside, out of his way, but he didn't head toward the door. He headed for her.

He wrapped his fingers around her upper arms in a grip that was surprisingly gentle, and sat her down on the window seat, then dragged a chair over in front of her. Sitting down, he took her hands in his.

Sunny shivered at their comforting warmth.

"The kidnapper called you, didn't he?"

"No, I—" Sunny squeezed her eyes shut. He was so sure, so strong. And she was so tired. It was so hard not to just tell him everything and let him help her. She shook her head.

His grip tightened. "Look at me."

She didn't want to meet his gaze, but something in his voice, something in the way he cradled her hands in his, made her feel safe.

"You may have fooled the officers, but you

aren't fooling me. I've been doing this for eight long years." His expression was solemn.

"You would never have opened your door to Burt Means. You were outside, and you weren't getting anything out of your car in a rainstorm in the middle of the night. He caught you outside because you were putting something *into* your car. Your packed a suitcase, your purse and Emily's diaper bag."

He rubbed his thumbs across her knuckles. "You were very lucky I was here. Otherwise, you might be in the clutches of a man who thinks you ruined his life and stole his child."

Sunny shuddered. He was too close. His hands holding hers felt too good. "What *were* you doing here?"

"I called to see if you were okay. You didn't answer."

Tears gathered in Sunny's eyes. She tried to pull away, but he held on.

"Now Means is out of the picture. He'll go back to prison for violating his parole. The police will check on him and Brittany, but I think you're right. He doesn't have Emily. The kidnappers called you, didn't they?"

"No, I—"

"Can the act, okay? I know you didn't receive a call on your house phone, or the police would have been notified. So the kidnapper called your cell phone. He gave you a meeting place or a drop place for the money. And of course he told you not to go to the police or the FBI."

"Please don't," she whispered. "Just leave me alone."

"I can't." Griff's intense violet gaze never wavered. "How did he get your cell phone number?"

She stiffened and tried to pull away. "I don't know."

Griff let go of her hands. He didn't want to bruise her. He'd hurt her enough.

She stood and turned around, folding her arms and bowing her slender shoulders. She'd changed her clothes, but her wet hair still hung in waves down past her collar.

Her muffled, anguished sobs ripped at his soul. He'd told her the truth. He'd been at this a long time. He'd comforted parents, reassured families and had borne the brunt of their fearful, helpless anger. But Sunny Loveless was worming herself into his heart in a way no one else ever had.

Something about her touched a sore, raw place deep inside him. A place he'd thought had scabbed over when he was fourteen.

Without considering the consequences, he reached for her. He slid his arm around her shoulders, prepared to offer the same reassurance he'd given time and time again in the past to so many terrified family members.

But as soon as his arm encircled her, the tension in her body melted and she turned toward him, her head bowed.

He pulled her closer, until she laid her cheek against his neck.

Griff bent his head, burying his nose in her wet hair. For a moment he stood quietly, feeling less alone than he'd ever felt. He squeezed his eyes shut.

This was an illusion and he had to get back to reality. "Emily had your cell number somewhere on her, didn't she? Was it sewn into her clothes? Engraved on one of her toys? Or maybe on a little bracelet?"

Sunny stiffened and pushed against his chest. Her silence confirmed his guess.

"I'm here to help you. I know how these people work."

She stepped backward, out of his reach, and hugged herself tightly.

"I don't want your help," she choked out. "I don't want the police's help. Can't you just leave me alone? Don't you have to go away if I don't want you?"

Chapter Six

If I don't want you. The words hit Griff surprisingly hard.

"No." He scowled, pushing away from her. "Kidnapping is a federal offense. It doesn't matter whether you *want* me or not. I don't have to go away. I can't. I'm bound by law to do everything possible to recover your child." He rubbed his chest. Her pain kept seeping past his defenses.

He cared about every case. He'd wept at the Senator's son's funeral. But he'd always managed to maintain a discreet distance from their deepest grief, so it wouldn't cloud his judgment.

But not this time.

Sunny's obstinacy and determination to protect her daughter ripped at his battle-scarred heart.

"Ms. Loveless, I know how frightened you are—" he started, his voice gruff.

She whirled, swinging her doubled fists at

him. "No you don't! You can't possibly know. She said these people are dangerous. They're capable of *anything!*"

"She?"

She shoved at him. "If you won't help me, get out of my way!"

In self-defense, Griff reached for her again, pinning her flailing arms to her sides.

"Let go of me!"

She fought his restraint with surprising strength.

"Shh," he whispered. "Shh. We'll find her. We'll save your baby. I swear."

"No you won't. You'll go bumbling in with your guns and sirens and the woman will run. I have to go alone."

"What woman, Sunny? Who is she? Where is she? Tell me. Let me help you."

She shook her head, flinging droplets of water from her hair into his face and over his arms.

"I don't know. All I know is—" She stopped dead still, then jerked away. "Let me go!"

He pulled her closer, his heart pounding at the feel of her supple body in his arms. The connection he'd felt between them the first moment he'd laid eyes on her warred with his sense of duty. He was bound by his badge to find her child, and he knew the best way to do that was to follow procedure, to use the FBI's tried-and-true methods and sophisticated technology. They worked.

Not always. Senator Chapman's ravaged face rose in his mind, and right behind it came the photo on his computer—the last picture he had of his baby sister.

Sunny quit struggling and went limp in his arms. She'd given up. He drew a deep, relieved breath. She was exhausted. She'd had next to no sleep since her baby had disappeared, and Means's attack had drained the last dregs of her energy.

But the thought of her admitting defeat cloaked him with unbearable sadness. He knew what she was feeling. The helplessness, the struggle against forces larger and stronger than she.

Damn it. He gritted his teeth. Why was it so easy to empathize with her? Why was he having to bite his tongue to keep from throwing logic to the wind and going with her to search for her child? He'd never considered anything like that before.

It had to be the city, and the memories it evoked.

"Emily needs me," she whispered against his neck, her breath warm, her tears at first hot, then quickly cooling against his sensitized skin.

The soft pressure of her breasts against his

chest and the clean wet scent of her hair tickling his cheek sent his blood surging. It was all he could do to keep from pressing a kiss to her temple.

To his dismay and disgust, his body hardened and stirred to life.

What a jerk he was, to react physically to her. She was a victim of a horrendous crime. She deserved his professionalism, his calm assurance and his help. Clenching his jaw, he gripped her upper arms and set her away from him.

She eyed him suspiciously. "Are you letting me go?" Her voice rose hopefully. She edged toward the door.

Meeting her tormented gaze, he felt something deep inside him crack, like a fissure running through an iceberg.

What he'd told Decker in the letter he'd left on his desk was true. He couldn't do this job anymore. It had become too personal.

He shook his head in defeat. "Sunny, I'll help you."

"I can't take the chance. The police will—"

"Sunny, listen. I mean me. *I'll* help you. We'll go together. Alone."

Her eyes widened, then narrowed. "I don't understand."

Neither did he. He'd had one dream ever since

his sister's disappearance. To become an FBI agent. He'd thought helping others would assuage his guilt and grief. And now he was about to step outside his own boundaries to chase a slender thread of hope for a woman he'd only known three days.

Whose hope was he trying to keep alive? Hers—or his own?

It was here, in Nashville, where he'd learned that holding on to hope could consume one's life. Was he dooming Sunny to the same sad fate? To years of charting the similarities in missing child cases? To sleepless nights devouring every tidbit of the latest abduction on the news channels? All in the forlorn belief that one day, one of those cases might provide a clue to the whereabouts of her child.

"Griff? What are you talking about? What do you mean you'll go with me?"

He rubbed his jaw and shrugged, working to act as if his decision was nothing more than an assessment of the situation, made through deliberation, not emotion.

"I've been thinking about what you said. You're right. Too much attention could spook the kidnapper. I think in this situation discretion might be better. If you'll trust me, I'll help you find Emily."

Sunny searched his face. For a second, the

private sadness she'd seen in his eyes the first time she'd met him was back. Something haunted him. Was it the ghosts of all the children he hadn't been able to save?

Despite her fear for her baby's safety, her easy compassion was stirred. He seemed driven by a private grief. Or was she merely transferring her own feelings to him? Maybe for him, it really was just a job—or maybe an obsession. Maybe he was one of those people who could not accept failure.

His reasons didn't matter. The only thing that mattered was whether she could trust him. What if she told him what she knew—gave him the woman's telephone number? Would he honor his promise? Would he help her? And did his definition of help match hers?

"Sunny? Will you trust me to go with you?"

Emily's pretty little face rose in her mind, innocent, wide-eyed, trusting. Her throat closed.

Sending up a prayer that she was doing the right thing, she squeezed her eyes shut for an instant, then nodded slowly, solemnly. "I don't have any choice."

"WELL NOW, this is interesting." Hiram couldn't believe his eyes, or his luck.

He'd spent the evening lurking around the hotel

where the FBI agent was staying, hoping he could get a chance to break into the agent's car. There had to be something in there that would tell him how much the agent knew, especially about Hiram's own involvement in the Loveless infant case.

But after it had started raining he'd holed up in his car, waiting for the deluge to stop. After about a half hour, he'd been ready to give up for the night. But just as he reached for the ignition switch, the agent had come running out.

At first Hiram had slunk down in his seat, scared silly that the man had spotted him and was coming after him. But he'd headed straight for his car, jumped in and taken off.

Hiram looked at the clock on his dashboard. It was late. Where was the agent going? After a moment's hesitation while he debated whether to follow or sneak into his room while he was gone, Hiram's curiosity won out. He started the car and tailed the agent.

It didn't take long for Hiram to realize that he was headed toward Sunny Loveless's house. Hiram's blood pressure rose, and he could hear his pulse hammering in his ears.

To avoid being seen, Hiram parked several houses away.

After watching for a while, he figured out that

the agent had surprised an intruder at Ms. Loveless's house. Then the police showed up with their sirens blaring, and lights popped on up and down the street. Hiram nearly fled, but all attention was concentrated on Sunny Loveless's house. Nobody noticed his old car.

If he had to guess, he'd bet that the man the police hauled away was Burt Means, the baby's biological father.

Then, the police took off, but the FBI agent didn't.

Afraid to move any closer, Hiram waited, squinting through the rain and wiping the fogged window glass with his handkerchief. He could barely make out shadowy movements behind the home's sheer curtains. Movements that indicated that the two people in the house were close—very close.

Hiram settled in and smiled. The tall, good-looking FBI agent was going to stay all night with the lovely, grieving mother. Hiram licked his lips and hoped there were sheer curtains in Ms. Loveless's bedroom.

But after a few minutes, to his amazement, the agent and Ms. Loveless came out, got into the agent's car and drove off.

Wondering if they were headed back to the agent's hotel, Hiram pulled out and followed them.

GRIFF RUBBED HIS NECK and yawned, trying his best to stay awake. He could barely keep his eyes open. He glanced at the dashboard clock. Almost three o'clock in the morning. He'd been up for twenty-four hours straight. He wasn't going to make it much farther without sleep.

The rain had stopped an hour or so before, but dense fog hung over the interstate, making misty haloes out of headlights and increasing the tendency toward road hypnotism.

He itched to call Natasha again, to see if she'd come up with anything on the two phone numbers Sunny had given him—the number the mysterious woman had used to call Sunny, and the number she'd been instructed to call once she got to Philadelphia. But he knew when Nat had information, she'd call him.

He glanced over at Sunny. She'd done her best to stay awake, but it was obvious how tired she was.

She had eyed him suspiciously until they'd driven out of the city on Interstate 40, fighting to keep her drooping eyelids open until she'd finally given in.

He couldn't blame her for having trouble believing that he was really skipping town with her in the middle of the night. He hardly believed it himself.

Watching her sleep replaced the seductive pull

of road hypnotism with an uncomfortable if pleasurable ache of longing, so for four hours he'd been dividing his attention between the rain-soaked road and her. She dozed fitfully, her body stiff with tension, her beautiful face marred by sadness.

She'd changed into snug-fitting jeans and running shoes, but she'd refused to take the time to dry her hair. Instead, she'd tucked it up on top of her head with some kind of barrette, and a few graceful waves had escaped to frame her face.

He reached over and brushed one long honeyed strand out of her eye, the tips of his fingers sliding over her petal-soft cheek.

The blare of a car horn jolted him, sending his heart slamming against his chest wall. He jerked the wheel, cursing under his breath. He'd almost drifted into the other lane.

Sunny sat up with a gasp. "What happened?" Her voice was low and husky.

"Nothing," he said shortly, willing his heartbeat to slow to normal as he rubbed his eyes. That was too careless. He had to have a couple hours' sleep.

"You're falling asleep at the wheel, aren't you? I'll drive."

As the pallid lights of Bristol, Tennessee,

came into view, Griff suppressed another yawn and stretched.

"No." Despite his denial, he took the next interstate exit, and pulled into the nearest motel, a mid-priced chain with few frills. The parking lot was full.

"What are you doing? Where are we?" Her voice sharpened.

"Bristol. I've got to get some sleep."

Sunny rubbed her eyes and yawned. "Bristol? We haven't even gone three hundred miles yet? No. We can't stop. You sleep while I drive."

He laughed shortly and shook his head. "Yeah, I don't think so. I haven't slept in twenty-four hours. How long has it been for you?"

"About fifteen seconds."

"You know what I mean. Lil said you haven't slept since Tuesday night."

"Lil worries about me."

"Somebody should."

"You can't stop. We've got to get to Philadelphia. Every minute counts."

"And we will, after I get a couple hours' sleep. Now, I'm going to register. I'll be right back."

Sunny seethed as she watched Griff stride into the motel lobby. If he'd left the keys in the car, she'd have thought seriously about driving away, but of course he hadn't. She should have insisted they bring her car. In fact, she should have flown. She'd have missed Burt's attack, and been in Philadelphia by now. But all she'd cared about was action. And truthfully, she was glad to have Griff with her. His solid strength made her feel confident that she would soon be holding her baby.

She shifted in her seat and groaned. Every muscle in her body ached. Her eyelids were so heavy she could barely focus.

Lil was right, and so was Griff. She hadn't slept. She couldn't, not while Emily's life rested in the hands of strangers.

Tears burned her aching eyes. No matter how determined she was, she knew she was reaching the breaking point. When she did close her eyes, she had odd dreams—maybe hallucinations.

She'd dreamed Griff had caressed her cheek. She touched the place where his fingers had brushed her skin—in her dream. A fierce longing streaked through her, surprising her with its intensity. His touch had felt so tender, so caring. The dream must have been her subconscious need for reassurance that he really cared about her and her baby, and not just his job.

The driver's door opened. Griff climbed in and started the engine. "There are only two rooms available. On opposite ends of the motel. Some car show in town." He pulled away from the motel entrance and drove toward the far end of the building.

Sunny suppressed a yawn. "I still say I can drive."

"No thanks. I don't want to wake up in a ditch because you went to sleep at the wheel."

"You actually think I'd fall asleep while driving toward my baby?"

"Staring at the road is hypnotic, especially if you're exhausted, which you are." He pulled into a parking place and cut the engine, then looked at her. "So indulge me."

"Indulge you. How long are you planning to sleep while my baby's life is in danger?"

He frowned in irritation, then held up the room key. "You're not going to do your baby any good if you end up in a car accident. Now, here we are. Number 14. No frills. No surprises."

Sunny frowned at the thought of settling between soft, clean sheets while Emily was missing. But oddly, for the first time since Emily had been taken, she felt as if she could relax. The thought that Griff would be close by gave her comfort. Somehow she knew he had her baby's best interests at heart.

"Great." She reached for the key. "Where's your room?"

Griff palmed the key, just out of her reach. "Right here. I'm not letting you out of my sight."

83 hours missing

GRIFF SQUINTED AT the clock radio on the bedside table. Nearly seven o'clock. He'd slept longer than he'd intended. His gaze slid past the clock to the other double bed, where Sunny lay, fully dressed except for her sneakers. She lay in a fetal position, her fists doubled up under her chin, as if she were holding fast to something precious. He hadn't had much of a chance to study her. Even watching her as she dozed in the car had been restricted to short glances at her shadowed face while he'd concentrated on the wet, foggy roads.

Feeling guilty for wasting time, he indulged himself for a few seconds. He didn't think he'd ever seen anyone so beautiful. Her hair was that brown-gold color of pure honey, and it draped over her cheek like a silken scarf. Her skin radiated wholesomeness, like the petals of a delicately hued rose.

Dark smudges marred the skin under her eyes—evidence of her worry and exhaustion. And the nasty bruises on her arms had grown to the size of half-dollars.

He should have gone with his first instinct and coldcocked Means for hurting her. He had the most uncharacteristic urge to lean over and kiss away the tiny frown between her brows, to brush his lips across her injured skin.

Who was he kidding? What he'd really like would be to pull her sleep-warmed body into his arms, and see those emerald eyes gleam with something other than sadness and suspicion.

He didn't know how to deal with the strong sexual attraction she evoked in him. He'd never felt anything but compassion and a secret kinship with the other people he'd helped. If someone had suggested three days ago that he would be lusting after a kidnapped baby's mother, he would have told them they were nuts.

Yet here he was, lying beside her in a shabby motel room, faintly disgusted at the direction his thoughts were taking, and yet at the same time growing more and more uncomfortable in his snug jeans.

Groaning silently, he eased out of bed. Quietly, he opened his leather computer case and retrieved his notebook computer. He set it on the minuscule desk and turned it on.

He'd check his e-mail and quickly run through the major news stories, in case there had been another kidnapping, or in case someone had already discovered he and Sunny were gone.

He glanced over at Sunny to be sure he hadn't awakened her, then slipped into the bathroom.

A hot shower and a quick shave made him feel

much better. He pulled on his jeans—not easy over his damp skin—and exited the bathroom.

Sunny was sitting at the tiny desk, staring at his computer. She turned her gaze on him, and he flinched at the furious glint in her eyes. "Sunny—"

"What is it?" Her voice cracked, and shock deepened the lines between her brows. Her gaze never wavered as she pushed her fingers through her sleep-tousled hair.

She'd opened the icon on his desktop labeled Missing Children.

"That's official business. You shouldn't—"

"What is this?" Her voice was as fragile as an old newspaper.

"It's a database. I use it—"

"What kind of a database?"

Griff swallowed. No one had ever seen his files before. Not even his boss, Decker. This was his private obsession. He'd kept information on every missing child case he'd ever heard of from the time he was fourteen—since his sister had disappeared. He'd started with notes jotted in a spiral notebook, then later on the computer.

"Never mind. It's obvious what it is. It's a list of child kidnappings." She tried to laugh, but her breath caught in the middle. "And look. Here's your latest entry. Date of disappearance—June 20, city—Nashville, abductee's name—Em-Emily Rose Loveless, age—six months." She rattled off the fields he'd set up, her voice becoming more and more brittle.

His face burned with shame. He should have been more careful. How awful for her to be confronted with her beloved child's name on a cold, impersonal computer screen.

His heart ached. How could she ever understand his need to catalog the dozens of successes and failures—not only his but others? His obsession with the methods and details of each case, in the hope that one day, he'd come across a case with enough similarities to his sister's disappearance that he could trace her whereabouts.

So he could finally find some closure.

"Oh, God—" Sunny's voice cracked like glass. "Disposition—recovered alive, recovered deceased, unsolved."

"Sunny, don't—"

"Emily's *disposition* is blank." She turned her haunted eyes on him. "You know, don't you?"

He shook his head. "Sunny, let me—"

"You know what will go in that space. Tell me. How long do you leave it blank? How long before you enter *unsolved* in that space?"

Griff swallowed. "Usually eight to twelve weeks."

He watched the color drain from her face.

"That doesn't mean the case is closed," he said quickly. "We never close a missing child case. You're looking at a working file I use to check on similarities, patterns. It was never meant to be seen by the families."

Sunny's eyes filled with tears. "I can see why," she said on a harsh little laugh. "Is this what you meant when you said it was just a job to you?"

Griff shook his head. He couldn't even put a name to all the turmoil inside him. It shattered him to watch her pain, to know he'd caused it. He already knew how she was going to feel each step of the way. How hope would grow inside like a balloon being filled with air, only to be deflated over and over again, by time, by disappointment, by failure.

"How far back does this list go? Ten years? Twenty? Thirty? Is there a listing of an abandoned newborn who was adopted by a kindly older couple here in Nashville almost thirty years ago?"

"Stop, Sunny. Don't do this to yourself."

She scrolled backward through the dates. "Do what to myself? Obsess over my missing baby? Wonder if the FBI knows anything about my birth parents?"

Griff stepped toward her. He had to stop her, for her sake, and for his. If she scrolled down very many more screens, she would see the first entry, his sister's.

"That list only covers fifteen years. There's nothing in there about you. As far as local records are concerned, there is no report of a newborn missing at the time of your birth."

"So you did check."

"Sure. It's my business."

Her face looked pinched. "Right. Your business."

She stood abruptly.

He breathed a sigh of relief that her attention was off his laptop, but then she walked toward him, her eyes bright with tears.

"I felt something in you," she said softly. "A sadness, an understanding. A need to save the children that went beyond just a job."

She placed her palm in the middle of his chest, branding the imprint of her hand into his skin.

"I thought you really cared."

She looked at her hand, then curled it into a fist and jerked it away.

Griff grabbed her wrist, trying to stop her, trying to force her to listen to him, but as soon as he touched her, she went rigid. She wasn't going to listen to anything he had to say. Not now. Maybe not ever.

He let go. "I do care, more than—"

Behind her, the computer screen flickered, and the screen saver came on—the photo of the Parthenon in Centennial Park that bright summer day fifteen years ago.

Griff pushed past her, reaching for the mouse. He moved it, stopping the slide show of photos of Marianne.

He was already in over his head with Sunny. He sure didn't want to explain about his sister.

Sunny turned as Griff's damp shoulder brushed her arm. His naked, curved back glistened with water droplets. Her fingertips already knew the texture of his skin, damp and warm from his shower. She'd felt the sleek, hard muscles of his chest, the faint rise of his pectorals. The fast, strong rhythm of his heart.

She rubbed her palm with her other thumb, wishing she'd never touched him, as her eyes traced the curve of his shoulders, the enticing bumpy trail of vertebrae down his back, the narrow glimpse of paler skin above the waistband of his jeans.

She fisted her hands as he maneuvered the mouse to close the database program.

It didn't matter. It was too late. She'd already seen the stark, impersonal list.

She couldn't describe, even to herself, how painful it was to see Emily's name there, just one among dozens of children over who knew how many years—some living, some dead, some still missing.

What she'd told him was true. She had felt a deep connection with him from the very beginning. His dark violet eyes were shadowed by a sadness that was more than just sympathy. She was certain he understood her pain, the way she understood the pain of the people who came to her for help.

But he worked with kidnappings on a daily basis. Maybe he'd developed a method designed to make frightened families trust him. Maybe it really was just a job to him.

When he straightened, a rivulet of water slithered down his spine to darken the waistband of his snug-fitting jeans. His lean back looked vulnerable, his skin still faintly pink from his shower, his wet hair curling a little at the nape of his neck.

To her dismay, her body tingled with a surprising need. Her fingers curled with the imagined feel of his sleek back. She swallowed, berating herself silently, about two seconds from asking him to please put on a shirt.

She needed a protector, a champion, a hardened lawman who could get the job done. Right now Griff Stone looked like a lover.

"You ready to go?" he asked.

She realized he was studying her, a curious glint in his eyes.

"No," she said shortly. "I need to shower. It won't take me but a few minutes."

"Yeah, right," he said, a small smile curving his lips.

She glared at him. "Time me," she snapped.

"It's okay. I need to check my e-mail and take a quick look at the news wires and the FBI alerts."

"Are you going to call Lieutenant Carver? Tell him where we are?"

"He'll be calling me soon enough. And you."

"What are we going to tell him?"

"I don't know."

"Please, tell me the truth."

Griff shrugged. "That is the truth. I'm going to call my boss first."

"Is that a good idea? I mean, you're not exactly following protocol, are you?"

"I think I can convince Decker to let me have a day or so, see what we find in Philadelphia."

Sunny wanted to beg Griff not to disclose their whereabouts to anyone, but she knew she couldn't push her luck.

Sunny went into the bathroom, which was still warm and humid from Griff's shower. She doffed her clothes and stepped under the shower's spray, letting the hot water sluice over her, washing grime and dust down the drain. She wished she could wash away the coating of fear and guilt that enveloped her. Fear that she would never see Emily again. Guilt that what her baby was going through was her fault.

Someone hated her so much that they would hurt her daughter to punish her.

As she quickly washed, she thought about Griff's computer, and whatever he had rushed to hide from her. As the hot, cleansing water sluiced over her, she prayed it wasn't bad news about Emily.

When she came out of the bathroom, Griff was on his cell phone.

Sunny's breath caught. Had Carver called? Had something happened?

"Great, Natasha. That's a big help. What about the other phone number?"

Sunny eavesdropped without shame as she squeezed water out of her hair with a towel.

He looked up, his gaze taking in her towel-draped hair, her jeans, and the little red top she'd pulled on.

Her skin was still damp from the shower and when his eyes lingered on the curve of her breasts, she felt them tighten.

"All right," Griff said. "So it'll take a while.

You've got my number. Call me as soon as you have something."

To hide her blush, Sunny patted her face with the towel for a few seconds. She tossed it back toward the bathroom then spoke. "That was your computer person?"

"Natasha." He nodded. "She has the location of the pay phone the woman used to call you. It's in a little town called Oak Grove, about half an hour east of Philadelphia. My boss has talked with Carver, who's coordinating with the locals there to check the phone booth."

"I thought it was going to be just you and me." She felt panic beginning to rise in her throat. "What if she's watching the phone booth?"

"She won't be. She'll be at home waiting for your call." Griff stood. "It is just you and me. But you knew I was calling about the phone numbers. Our best strategy is to locate the woman and talk to her in person."

"You mean don't warn her we're coming. She promised she'd give me Emily, and I promised to come alone."

Griff saw Sunny's eyes grow wider and darker as her fear spiraled out of control. He stepped over and put his arm around her.

Her shoulders felt thin and fragile under his larger, stronger arm. A fine trembling gripped her, underlying a rigidity that he knew was grown from fear.

"Calm down, Sunny," he whispered. When had he started calling her Sunny? He'd vowed to keep his distance. And her name brought him too close. "Natasha has contacts. The number the woman gave you is for a prepaid cell phone."

Her voice was muffled. "If she can find out who sold it, the seller can give us the woman's name and address."

"That's right."

"But if the woman sees the police—" her breath hitched "—she'll run."

Griff tightened his embrace. "You've got to trust me."

Then for the first time, Sunny slipped her arms around his waist and buried her face in the curve of his neck. "Just please get Emily back for me."

He touched her hair, its damp coolness a shock to his heated skin. Bending his head until his lips brushed her hair, he whispered, "I promise you I will. I promise."

Dear God, he hoped the woman wasn't leading them into a trap.

HIRAM SWITCHED ON his windshield wipers again. The wiper motor struggled to life. The blades dragged noisily over the wet glass. Damn summer rain. On again, off again. If his wipers quit working once more, he'd be blind.

It had been a long night, watching the motel room's door, to be sure neither Sunny nor the FBI agent left.

They had to have gotten a call. Probably from Bess Raymond.

Ed had told him that Janie had taken the Loveless baby to Bess. That was a mistake, in his opinion. He'd never met the woman who kept Janie's babies. But he figured she'd been as relieved as he had when Ed and Janie had gotten out of the baby-selling business.

Then, like him, Bess had been jerked back into it. He wouldn't be surprised if her conscience was eating at her. He could understand how she felt.

But he needed the money. Conscience didn't pay the bills.

The motel room door opened. It was the agent, bringing out two bags. He turned around and said something to Sunny, then headed for the metal stairs leading down to the parking lot.

Good. They were on the road again. As soon as he could verify where they were headed, he'd call Janie. He wanted to be sure. He didn't want to give Janie the wrong information. That could be bad for his health.

The rain got heavier as Sunny came out.

Hiram turned the wipers to high and listened to them stumbling over the glass as he cranked his car.

"Come on, old girl," he muttered to his ancient Plymouth. "We're back on the scent."

"HOW CAN THE COFFEE be burned at nine o'clock in the morning?" Griff asked as he poured a cup.

"Probably because that machine hasn't been cleaned since it was installed."

He chuckled at the faint lift in Sunny's voice. He hadn't seen her smile yet, but she sounded more upbeat than she had in the four days he'd known her. "I notice it's not stopping you from having a cup."

She made a face at him. "Only because there's no other choice."

"We could have had breakfast at that restaurant—"

"No." She pressed her lips together. "We've wasted enough time."

Griff nodded. He agreed. He'd hoped to be well on their way before now. He expected a phone call from Lieutenant Carver any second, berating him for not notifying the police of the phone call.

He laid the packaged sweet roll and bag of

chips next to the yogurt smoothie Sunny had picked up on the convenience store's counter. "That all you're having?"

She looked down at his items then up at him, her brows arched.

"Point taken," he acknowledged, and laid his left hand over her proffered bill as he handed the clerk a twenty. "I've got it."

She slipped her hand from under his and took a small step away. "Thanks," she said.

He glanced over at her but she dropped her gaze, busy returning the bill to a pocket of her purse.

He grabbed the bag and the coffees, handing one cup to her as they exited the store.

Even though it was raining, he slid on his sunglasses and glanced around as Sunny climbed into the passenger side of the rental car. His gaze lit on an old, dark green Plymouth parked on the far side of the convenience store parking lot.

It was the same car that had been parked at the motel. Griff was certain of it. He recognized the dent in the left front fender. He squinted. There was a front tag, which told him the car was from Tennessee. He was too far away to make out the numbers through the misty rain.

There was someone in the driver's seat but he couldn't see anything but a dark, shapeless form.

He debated whether to just walk over and confront the driver. But he didn't want to endanger Sunny, nor did he want any further delay.

He'd just give them a run for their money and see if they could keep up. If they did, he'd snag their license plate and call it in.

After handing the sack of food to Sunny, Griff climbed into the driver's seat and pulled away. He turned back toward the motel.

"The interstate is north of here," Sunny said, peeling the perforated tab off the lid of his coffee.

"Yep. I want to check something."

"What?"

Griff didn't answer. As he pulled into the right-hand lane, he glanced in the rearview and side mirrors. The green Plymouth followed suit, two cars back.

They were being followed.

"Hold on." He took a quick right onto a side street, then an immediate left.

"We're being followed?" She tried to look behind her.

"Hang on. Watch the coffee."

At the next street, he whipped the wheel to the right at the last second and then turned right again. He watched the rearview mirror but couldn't see the green car. He headed back toward the interstate.

Beside him, Sunny blotted up spilled coffee with a napkin.

"Are you burned?"

"No, no thanks to you." She dried off the cup and placed it in the cup holder nearest him. "Who was that?"

Griff checked the mirrors as he guided the car onto the entrance ramp of the interstate.

"I don't know. A green Plymouth. Old." Finally satisfied that there was no sign of the green Plymouth, he pulled onto I-91 and relaxed minutely.

"Ever seen a beat-up green Plymouth hanging around?"

"No. What about the license?"

"Couldn't see it, but there was a front plate."

"Tennessee."

"Yeah." He took a sip of his coffee. "Ugh! Maybe we shouldn't drink this. I want to get as far away from here as possible before we have to stop. How long can you hold out?"

"As long as you can." Sunny's voice rang with determination.

Out of the corner of his eye, Griff saw her fingers tremble as she pushed them through her hair. The idea of being followed had spooked her. She wasn't as calm and composed as she was pretending to be.

She was terrified, but she had courage. Maybe as much as anyone he'd ever met. And her emerald eyes burned with the fire of hope.

He prayed he wouldn't have to be the one to snuff that fire.

Chapter Seven

96 hours missing

"I don't care what time it is." Sunny glared at Griff. "That woman has Emily. I'm not spending another night without my baby. She said to call her when I got to Philadelphia. Well, we're here. I'm going to call her." To her dismay, her eyes filled with tears and her pulse pounded.

She dug into her purse for her cell phone, but her vision blurred and the purse slipped out of her fingers and onto the floorboard.

"Yeah, we're here, and it's ten o'clock at night. Look at you. You're so tired you can't even hold on to your purse. We're only a few minutes outside of Oak Grove. We'll get some sleep, and first thing in the morning, I'll contact the local police and Natasha. We need to be prepared."

Frustration burned in her chest. "Prepared? For what? The woman is waiting for me to call her. She has my baby."

Griff exited the interstate and headed for a motel.

"Why won't you listen to me?"

Griff didn't answer. She glanced over at him and saw a sad look in his eyes.

We need to be prepared.

"You think *she's* the kidnapper." Her heart slammed painfully in her chest. She pressed her palm against her diaphragm. "You think that was Jane Gross who called?"

"No. The police in New York questioned Jane and Edward Gross today. Gross is running for Congress, and last night they were at a charity function with the other candidates."

"But that doesn't mean they couldn't have called."

"I know. But they've lawyered up and threatened to sue for defamation of character. And anyhow it doesn't make sense."

"Why should it?" Sunny asked wearily. "Nothing else has."

Griff squeezed her knee. "My gut tells me the woman who called you is sincere. She really does want to get Emily back to you. I just don't want to make any mistakes."

Sunny's eyes brimmed over with tears that

streamed down her face when she blinked. "Thank you."

His dark eyes softened and his fingers on her knee tightened reassuringly. "Don't cry, Sunny," he whispered. "Do you trust me?"

She nodded, surprised to discover that she did. He might be just doing his job, but his integrity and sincerity burned in the violet flame of his eyes.

She prayed that her trust wasn't misplaced.

A COUPLE OF HOURS LATER, Griff had showered, and was sitting in front of his laptop, dressed in jeans and nothing else, comparing the various elements of Sunny's case to other cases in his database. It was a frustrating pastime. There were few similarities beyond the expected ones. She'd been alone. There had been no ransom request. It was unusual to see a physical confrontation.

Which was the main reason Griff was sure Emily had been taken either for revenge or for leverage.

He sorted the database to see how many other cases he had recorded that began with an attack. Only six. Three of those were family members. The other two, besides Sunny's case, were unbalanced women who swore the children were theirs.

He sighed and raked his fingers through his

wet hair, then sorted by city, although he already knew how many cases had occurred in Nashville. Just two. He stared at them.

A hesitant knock sounded at the connecting door between their rooms.

Sunny. He jumped up and flung open the door. "What is it? Are you all right?"

She stood there, in a pink tank top and drawstring pajama pants, her hair caught up with a clip, and tears overflowing her eyes.

She was clutching something in her hands. "I'm sorry, Griff, but I couldn't stand it anymore. I called the number."

"Damn it!" He slapped his palm against the wall. "What'd you do that for? Didn't I explain—?"

"Yes. Intellectually I knew it was a bad idea. But I'm having a really hard time listening to my logical side right now." A tiny laugh escaped her lips as her eyes glowed with tears. "It doesn't matter anyway. There was no answer. She's gone. She took Emily and ran."

"Hey." Griff held out his arms and she walked right into them, still clutching the cell phone in front of her.

Silent sobs erupted like little earthquakes through her body. "I'm sorry. I should be stronger," she whispered.

"You're doing great," he whispered, his heart

breaking for her. It had taken him weeks to realize Marianne was never coming back. At fourteen, hope had lasted much longer.

"Emily is fine. She has to be." He pulled her over to the bed and sat down with her. He pulled her into his arms, clenching his jaw against the feel of her soft skin against his bare chest and shoulders. "Didn't you tell me the woman sounded kind and loving?"

God, what was he doing? He was lying to her, breaking his own code of honor. He'd never lied to a family, never given them false hope. He'd always been kind, gentle, but realistic.

He had no idea whether they would find Emily, or what might have happened to her. But suddenly, the most important thing to him was Sunny. He had to find Emily. He wouldn't be able to live with himself if he let Sunny down.

But he had a problem. A big one.

No matter how many times he went over the evidence, he still couldn't make the pieces of the puzzle fit together.

He was counting on the woman who'd called Sunny to fill in the missing pieces.

He gently took the cell phone from her unresisting fingers.

"I screwed up, didn't I?"

"I should have taken your phone away from you yesterday." He was the one who had screwed up. It was a critical error on his part. Now the woman was warned. She knew Sunny was here.

A tiny, ironic laugh escaped Sunny's lips. "That wouldn't have stopped me. There's a phone in my room."

Griff berated himself silently. *Of course*. The only way he could have stopped her from making the call was to stay in the same room with her and watch her constantly. But he hadn't wanted to suffer through another night lying next to her, unable to touch her.

"You need to sleep. We're going to have a busy day tomorrow. No matter where the woman is, as soon as Natasha has an ID from that cell phone number, we'll find her."

"What if we don't? What if the woman is just some crank? What if this is a wild-goose chase?" Sunny buried her face in her hands. "I can't sleep. I can't eat. I keep seeing Emily alone, hungry, sick. What if they're hurting her? What if she's in the hands of some sick—" She stopped.

"Sunny—"

"What if she's already dead?"

Griff could have recited all the what-ifs right along with her. He'd heard them all. Hell, he'd *said* them all. And he knew, too, that the more time that went by, the more real the what-ifs became.

He wrapped his fingers carefully around her arms and set her a little away from him, then lifted her chin with a finger. "Listen to me. You have to stop thinking like that. You have to sleep and eat. You have to be strong, because *when* we find Emily, she's going to need her mother."

Her eyes implored him. "Tell me I'll see her again."

He pulled the covers back and patted the pillow. "Come on, get into bed. I'll turn the lights out."

With a wary look at him, Sunny obeyed. She climbed under the covers and lay down. Her deep, shaky sigh told him how exhausted she was.

He turned off the lamp, leaving the room in darkness, except for the pale blue glow of his laptop screen. He powered it down and closed it.

"Griff?"

"Yeah?"

"Tell me."

A lump rose in his throat. The urge to promise her she'd see her baby tomorrow was overwhelming, but he bit his tongue.

No more empty lies. Hadn't he learned to hate the smooth-talking FBI agents and detectives who'd kept promising him and his dad that they'd find Marianne? Even as a young teen, he'd known they were lying. It hadn't stopped him from believing them. But he'd always sworn to be honest with the families.

He looked down at Sunny, curled up, her closed eyes damp with tears. Giving in to a yearning he'd suppressed since the first time he'd seen her, he leaned over and kissed her forehead gently. "You go to sleep. Tomorrow we'll talk to Natasha. We're close. Very close."

He straightened and swallowed, but the lump was still there. He turned toward the connecting door.

"Griff?"

"Yeah?"

"You're not going to leave me, are you?"

He sighed. How could he tell her no? How could he stand to stay? "Of course not. I'll be right here."

"You can lie down on the bed, too."

Her sleepy, sexy voice sent thrills rushing through him, but he clenched his jaw, angry at himself. Her words stirred his body to life in a way that would shock her if she knew. But she was terrified and exhausted. If his presence would help her sleep, how could he refuse?

He was a master of control. It was a requirement in his business. He would never betray her trust that way. No matter how much his body ached for her. She was too scared, too vulnerable. Too close.

"I'll just sit—"

"Please?"

He grimaced, and rubbed his eyes. "Okay," he said reluctantly. He lay down on top of the covers, still in his jeans.

A soft sigh drifted past his ears like the breeze from a butterfly's wing, and he felt Sunny's tense body relax. Before long, her even breaths told him she'd fallen asleep.

He lay stiffly, careful to stay on his side of the bed, and trying not to move too much. He didn't have a prayer in hell of falling asleep, but he didn't want to chance waking her.

So he lay there, wanting her with an aching need that throbbed through him with every beat of his heart, and waited for morning.

BURT HAD HER. Sunny struggled with all her strength, but he'd wrapped her up in something. She couldn't breathe, couldn't move. All she could do was scream.

"Sunny."

He touched her face.

No! Get off me! I swear I don't know where Emily is!

Then suddenly, Griff was there, big and strong and safe. He tossed Burt into an iron cage and held out his arms to her.

"You're safe now. I'll carry you," he said. "We're close."

"Sunny, wake up."

She curled her fingers against hot silky skin. The smell of soap and cinnamon swirled around her, a safe, yet exciting scent. The scent of strength and goodness.

"Sunny, it's me, Griff. You were having a bad dream."

The words finally penetrated her dream-soaked brain. "Griff?"

She felt his heart beating fast and strong. Felt his rapid breathing.

"I dreamed about Burt. He was going to kill me."

"He's in custody. You're here with me. Safe."

"Safe. That's what you said." She made a sad little sound that could as easily have been a sob. "I'm safe. But what about Emily?"

Suddenly, she couldn't bear it any longer—the uncertainty, the fear for Emily's safety, the horror of losing her baby. She broke down, all the locked-up grief and tension pouring out in uncontrollable sobs.

"Oh, God. I can't do this. I can't keep pretending." The bedclothes were tangled around her, suffocating her. She pushed against them and leaped out of bed.

Griff was there, beside her. "Sunny, you're still in the dream. You need to wake up. Come on, everything's going to be fine."

"No! No!" She pushed at him. "Stop it! Don't lie to me! You haven't lied to me before. Don't lie now."

But he had. Griff's heart thudded painfully in his chest. He'd lied to her every day, every minute. He'd never told her why he'd been chosen to work on her case.

"Come on. Let's get you back in bed." He held out his arms.

"No!" She slapped at his hands. "Get away from me. I can't sleep."

She paced back and forth, like a caged tiger. "Maybe I should look at your database. We should send it to Lil. She's really good at finding patterns. Maybe—" Her voice broke.

Her pain dug into him. He couldn't bear to see her so heartbroken. He couldn't bear to see her trying so hard to hold on to control.

To his surprise, her knees gave way and she crumpled to the floor. She wrapped her arms around her knees and lowered her head, her slender back shaking.

Griff sat down on the floor beside her and gently pulled her into his arms. She didn't resist.

After a while, her sobs quietened, then turned to an occasional little snuffle.

He blinked away the dampness from his own eyes, and stood, urging her up with him.

"Come on, let's go to sleep. You need your strength for tomorrow. Remember, you're going to see Emily."

She felt breakable. It hurt him.

Guiding her over to the bed, he pulled back the tangled covers. "There you go. I'll tuck you in."

"Don't." Her voice was small but firm.

"Okay." He brushed her hair away from her face with a hand that wasn't totally steady. He'd comforted dozens of families through these times when their faith ran out and their hope faded, but Sunny's breakdown had crushed his already sore heart.

His fingers lingered on her cheek for an instant, then he straightened.

"I'm going to—"

"Hold me. Please?"

He glanced at her in surprise. The little pink top she wore for sleeping outlined her small, perfect breasts. Her skin gleamed like porcelain in the dim light from the windows; her hair had dried wavy and soft, and floated around her head and shoulders like angel hair.

She was the most beautiful being he'd ever laid eyes on. He couldn't touch her. He couldn't trust himself to.

"That's not a good idea."

"Please. Please just stay here. You don't know what I see when I close my eyes. I can't do it alone."

He did know. Too well. He squeezed his eyes shut, telling himself he was strong enough to bury his feelings. He could be a comfort to her. He could hold her and make her feel safe, the way no one had for him when his sister disappeared.

He sat down on the bed.

"I'm so cold. So scared. I can't stop shaking. I can't stop thinking about her."

He realized he was shaking, too. He was finding it harder and harder to pretend she was just another terrified family member he was bound to help. She was becoming so much more. His body was already hard just from the thought of holding her close.

He would do anything for her, but he didn't want to hold her. Once he touched her, he knew with an awful certainty he'd never be the same again.

Sunny saw the reluctance in his face. And the fear. She was afraid, too. She felt the life draining out of her, felt grief sucking away her strength. She needed something to draw on.

And Griff was the strongest, most honorable man she'd ever met.

"Make me feel safe." She stared up at him, holding his gaze, until he blinked. She knew he'd lost the battle with himself.

He turned off the lamp.

Dim light filtering through the motel curtains outlined the shape of his body. Lean and long, with sleek, sharply planed muscles.

He slid into bed beside her and as naturally as if they'd been lovers for years, she slipped into the curve of his arm.

Pressing her cheek against the hollow between his shoulder and neck, she rested her hand on his chest and released a shuddering sigh.

"Sunny—" He stiffened.

"I'm sorry," she whispered, and pulled her hand away.

"It's okay." He wrapped an arm around her shoulders, and let the fingers of his other hand brush her forearm. Then he slid his fingers down her arm to her wrist, then to her hand. He picked it up and pulled it to his lips, then lay it on his chest.

Oh, it felt so good, to be held, to be cherished.

The promise of his strong, sleek body against hers gave her what words never would. They gave her the strength to believe.

She didn't care if she was stealing it from him.

Didn't care if the confidence and safety weren't rightly hers. She'd take what she could get.

Tears gathered in her eyes as she relaxed against him. "You're a good man, Griffin Stone."

She felt his head shake. "No. No, I'm not. I'm trying to be."

She turned her head and buried her nose in the hollow of his shoulder, letting her lips brush his skin. It was a small theft, just a tiny sense of the tantalizing mixture of strength and gentleness that characterized him.

He drew a sharp breath, and before she realized what she was doing, Sunny slid her hand around his neck.

His head bent and hers raised and their lips barely brushed each other, like the wake of a butterfly's wing.

Inside her, something incredible happened. The feel of his mouth on hers was indescribable. His lips tasted like a healing potion.

At first he was hesitant, barely touching her, as if he thought she would break. But Sunny didn't feel fragile.

She felt dazed and light-headed. She liked the feeling. It took away her fear, even if for a moment. She wanted to be filled, surrounded by him.

She deepened the kiss, and he growled in his throat, the sound vibrating through his lips.

A sensual thrill centered inside her, all the way down to the core of her sexuality.

He felt it, too. She knew he did because he slid down in the bed, pulling her with him, and stretched his body against hers. His hand reached around to cup her bottom and pull her close.

He wanted her. His body told her so.

The thought strengthened the throbbing yearning that engulfed her.

His body hardened, and he pressed against her, his erection hot, pulsing against her thighs as he took her mouth, then trailed his lips and tongue down her neck.

"I should stop," he whispered raggedly against the hollow of her throat. "This isn't right. You don't want this." He lifted his head and stared deep into her eyes, his so dark they looked black. "You just want comfort."

She cupped his cheek with her hand. "I do want it. I want you. I need you." She pulled his head back down and kissed him again, arching against him in a growing frenzy of need.

Griff moaned quietly and touched her, his fingers trailing heat over her skin as he slid her pajamas off.

His skin glided against hers, steel against silk. His heat warmed her fear-chilled body. His strength surrounded her. For this moment at least, she felt hope.

When he raised himself above her, she ran her hands up his sinewy arms to his broad shoulders, then encircled his neck. He slid into her with sweet agonizing slowness.

With a moan, Sunny arched, seeking more.

His breathing grew erratic. She felt his heart beating through his whole body, and hers sped up, matching his rhythm.

He sank hilt deep, filling her, giving her a sense of completion she'd never before felt.

Then he began to move, and a tremor built inside her. From her core, a wondrous tension built with agonizing, titillating slowness, until she wanted to scream with anticipation.

Just when she thought she couldn't stand it any longer, he stiffened and strained against her, plunging again and again, driving her past all thought. His release triggered hers, and she reached her own nearly unbearable pinnacle just seconds after his.

105 hours missing

THE MORNING SUN shone in Hiram's eyes as he looked across the street from the motel at his ancient Plymouth, sitting in the holding lot of the auto repair shop next door. The old girl had given him two hundred and seventy thousand miles of uncomplaining service over the past twelve years.

But now she was a goner, and he was stuck seventy miles outside of Philadelphia, and it was all Janie Gross's fault. If she'd just answered her phone. He'd tried to call her three times last night to let her know that Sunny Loveless and the FBI agent were headed toward Bess's.

The last time he'd called, while the tow truck was hauling his car back here, he'd dared to leave a message. Nothing specific. Just *you'd better call me*.

Turning away from the window, he looked at his watch and thought about calling Janie again, for the *last* time. He needed money, now more than ever, but he'd about decided being homeless on a street corner in the middle of winter would be better than putting up with Janie's nutty paranoia.

His cell phone rang.

"This better be good, Hiram." Janie's hoarse voice scraped his raw nerves. "I told you not to call me."

Hiram couldn't help but grin. She was going to regret talking to him like that. He made a point of sounding apologetic. "I didn't mean to bother you, Janie, but I thought you'd like to know that the last I saw of Sunny Loveless and her FBI agent, they were in his car, headed up Interstate 95."

"What! Why didn't you—" Janie cut off in the middle of her tirade.

Hiram knew what she was about to say. *Why didn't you call me?* But he had. She had three missed calls on her cell phone. She couldn't blame him.

"Yeah, and now my car's broke down. I'm about seventy miles east of Philly. I'm going to need you to wire me some money so I can get her fixed."

"Screw you and your car. Bess must have figured out whose baby she had. She must have called her. Damn that old hag. I've got to get there before they do."

She cut the connection.

Hiram looked at his cell phone, thinking about Janie's words. A sick lump of fear lodged in his chest. Janie wouldn't hurt a baby—would she?

His mind made the next logical leap. How much trouble would he be in if he turned her in? Surely the police and the FBI would appreciate knowing exactly who had kidnapped the Loveless woman's baby girl, not to mention the dozens of other children Janie and Ed had brokered over the years.

They might be willing to pay for the information. With his information, they could solve dozens of crimes. That ought to be worth something.

THE HARSH JANGLE of a phone woke Sunny. For an instant, she was disoriented. Someone stirred next to her, and the memory of Griff's strong hot body enveloping hers slid through her with a thrill.

He groaned under his breath and sat up as the phone rang again, louder.

Opening her eyes to a squint, she saw the sleek curve of his naked back, lean broad shoulders and dark hair that was tousled and curling at the nape of his neck.

"Yeah?" his gravelly voice reverberated through the thin mattress of the double bed. "Hey, Natasha, whatcha got?"

Emily. Shame sucker punched Sunny. She was naked, in bed with the FBI Agent who was helping her find her daughter.

Dear God, what kind of mother was she? She'd indulged herself while Emily was lost, possibly in danger.

For the first time in the entire six months she'd been Emily's mother, her first thought upon waking was not of the child she'd sworn to love and protect. Her heart gaped with aching emptiness.

I'm so sorry, Emily Rose.

Griff stood and pushed his fingers through his hair. He bowed his head and scratched the back of his neck, yawning.

"Yeah, we're up." He sent her a sheepish grin that lit his face and made his oddly colored eyes sparkle.

Sunny sat up, pulling the sheet with her. She couldn't breathe. Had they found Emily?

"Bergen Street in Oak Grove, seventeen miles west of Philadelphia. Okay, got it." He reached over and picked up Sunny's cell phone off the bedside table, flipped it open and deftly pressed keys. "Yeah, here it is. That's the same number."

"They've found her?" Sunny touched him on the forearm.

Griff laid his hand over hers as he spoke into the phone. "No. Absolutely not! I don't care what CAC says. They asked me to be in charge of this case. They can't—" He cut himself off, then took a swift breath. "Let me talk to Decker."

Where were her pajamas? Her face burned with humiliation. She'd never done anything like this in her life. She found them and slipped them on, while her mind raced.

What was going on? CAC was Crimes Against Children. She knew that from her investigative work. It was a special division of the FBI devoted to missing children.

She remembered someone saying that Griff was with a different division of the FBI, but Griff had assured her that he was an expert in missing child cases. So she hadn't questioned why CAC wasn't involved. She'd been too distraught about Emily.

"What's wrong?" she asked him.

He lifted his head and looked at her from under his lashes. Her hand covered her skimpy, revealing tank top.

"I'm going to be a few minutes here," he said, his gaze flickering toward her hand. "Why don't you go get dressed? We've got the address of the woman who called you."

"Oh—" Sunny's heart stopped, then thudded against her chest. Her throat spasmed. Joy and relief washed over her and brought tears to her eyes. She *would* get to see Emily today. Hold her, kiss her, smell her sweet baby hair.

She looked at Griff through tear-blurred eyes.

"Thank you," she whispered. She loved Griffin Stone at that moment. He'd kept his promise. He'd found her baby. With one hand over her mouth, she laid her other hand against his face.

Griff winced at the tender feel of Sunny's hand on his cheek and the hope and joy shimmering in her eyes.

It terrified him and sent a spear of guilt lancing

through his chest. He'd taken advantage of her last night, and today he felt like a heel. But as bad as he felt, he couldn't take his eyes off her. The little pajama thing she wore made her look fragile and feminine, although she'd felt anything but fragile last night.

Griff swallowed hard and tried to banish the memories of her firm, supple body under his, meeting his need with a need of her own that had surprised him.

Right now, he had to deal with the head of CAC, who was angry that Griff had run off with the baby's mother on what he considered a wild-goose chase—and a dangerous one at that. So he needed her out of his sight. He couldn't afford to be distracted. Besides, he didn't want her to hear his conversation with Decker.

He tried to smile reassuringly at Sunny, and the answering smile she sent him lit up the room like a cake full of birthday candles. A spear of dread pierced his heart.

He'd done what he'd sworn he'd never do. He'd gotten his heart involved. He'd promised her he would find her baby, knowing he had no right to get her hopes up.

How many promises was he going to make, before he found one he could keep?

"Go on," he said gently.

As she stepped through the connecting door, he couldn't take his eyes off her. She was so beautiful, so brave. So trusting.

"Griff?" A strong, steady voice sounded in his ear.

"Mitch."

"Everything okay?"

Typically, Decker didn't offer recriminations. He merely listened to the facts and gave his input. Griff knew it was up to him to give Decker the information he needed.

"It appears the woman who has the child is not the kidnapper. Ms. Loveless was contacted and told to come to Philadelphia, then contact the woman for further instructions on how to get her baby back."

"I see." There was a world of concern behind those two words. Griff knew Decker was assessing his ability to handle the case, given his uncharacteristic actions.

"Evidence that she's not the kidnapper?"

"Nothing, sir, except Sun—Ms. Loveless's report of what the woman said."

"How confident are you?"

Griff thought about all the tidbits of information, not much of which added up. Then he thought about Sunny's determination.

With or without him, Sunny would have made this trip.

"Sir, I felt it was my duty to protect Ms. Loveless."

Decker didn't speak.

Griff was reminded of rumors he'd heard about Decker and his wife. About how the honorable, unflappable Special Agent in Charge had acted out of character a couple of years ago in order to protect the woman who was now his wife from a murderer.

"Mitch, this feels right. Let me follow through with it. Hell, this will probably be the last favor I ever ask of you. You saw my letter of resignation? I left it on your desk."

"Regretfully, I did. I was hoping you'd change your mind."

Bowing his head, Griff rubbed his chest. "No. That won't happen. Coming back to Nashville cemented my decision. This will be my last case for the FBI. I can't do this anymore."

"Find that little girl, Griff, but call for backup. The local field agent is standing by, as is local law enforcement. I'll deal with CAC."

Griff took down the names and numbers of the locals.

Detecting a movement out of the corner of his eye, Griff turned. Sunny stood at the adjoining door to their rooms. Her shocked expression told him she'd heard every word.

She'd just discovered that her precious daughter's life was in the hands of an FBI agent who wanted out.

Griff thanked Decker and disconnected. Without looking at Sunny, he reached for his T-shirt and pulled it over his head. "Ready to go?"

"You're quitting the FBI?" Her voice accused him. "What about Emily?"

"We don't have much time." Chalk up one more reason he needed to get out. He was becoming way too emotionally involved with this case. *With Sunny,* a small voice in his head whispered.

"I don't understand. A few days ago you told me it was *just a job and you were good at it.*"

He reached for his shirt, using the process of buttoning it to avoid looking at her.

She took a step toward him. "So if it's just a job, why can't you do it anymore?"

He glanced up. He knew what she was feeling. In her mind, she'd just been abandoned by the one person who had sworn to take her shattered world and make it right again.

He still remembered the day he and his father had been told that there were no leads in his sister's disappearance and how bereft he'd felt as the tall, stoic agent had walked away.

He straightened, meeting her gaze. "I'm not quitting today."

Chapter Eight

Janie drove like hell toward Oak Grove, seething. She didn't know how much time she had to get to Bess, but she sure as hell wasn't wasting any of it.

She'd thrown some lie at Ed about her mother being sick. He'd have to make his appearance at church today without her. She had to get her hands on that baby before Sunny Loveless got there. The kid was her ace in the hole. She had an alternate babysitter lined up in New York City, a woman she'd used a couple of times in the past.

All she had to do was get the kid, drop it off in New York, then get back to New Rochelle before tomorrow morning, when Eddie and she were scheduled to meet with their lawyer and Ed's campaign manager. They had to work on a plan to deflect the bad publicity caused by the landlord's death.

Ashes flew from her cigarette as she slapped

the steering wheel with her palm. This was all Hiram's fault. He'd been such an idiot through all this—calling her about insignificant things, unable to make a decision for himself. She'd gotten sick of his whining.

How in hell was she supposed to know that *this* time, his phone call was vitally important?

She turned into the street behind Bess's house, and parked in the backyard, as she always did, breathing a sigh of relief that the only other vehicle was Bess's old pickup.

Taking the .22 that Ed had given her years ago from her glove compartment and slipping it into her purse, Janie walked around to the front door. As she passed the child's sandbox, she flicked her cigarette into it. Finally, a use for a kid's plaything.

When Bess opened the door, the old woman didn't even look surprised to see her.

That shocked her. Her head began to pound. Had Loveless already been here and gone?

Janie didn't waste any time on pleasantries. "I'm here for the kid." She pushed past Bess and into the living room. "Where is she?"

"Janie, I've done your bidding for years, against my better judgment. When you showed up here fifteen years ago, with that precious child—"

Janie whirled. "Oh spare me, you old hag!" She took out a cigarette.

Bess frowned. "I've asked you not to smoke in the house."

"Screw you." She pointed with the unlit cigarette. "Get the kid, now. I've got to get out of here."

Bess folded her arms. "I don't have her."

"You—" The fear that ate at her gut turned into panic. "What have you done?" The cigarette broke in her fingers. "Has Sunny Loveless been here?"

"Who?"

"Don't mess with me! You know who she is. You called her, didn't you? *Didn't you!*"

"Yes, I called Ms. Loveless."

"What the hell were you thinking? You're in this as deep as I am."

"Not as deep, Janie, and not anymore."

Janie muttered curses as she stalked through the small house, scanning every room with a growing sense of dread. Bess didn't follow.

Back in the living room, Bess still stood in the same position, her arms folded, a serene expression on her face. "I told you, I don't have her."

Rage burned in Janie's ears and a sizzling pain penetrated her left temple like a hot skewer. Her fists clenched.

"And I asked you a question." She advanced on Bess and grabbed her arm. "Did Loveless already take it?"

A disgusted look darkened Bess's face, and a

still certainty surrounded her. "I won't tell you anything else. Get out of my house."

Janie pushed Bess. "Where is she?" She doubled her fist and raised it, but Bess stood her ground, unflinching.

"There's nothing you can do. This stops here and now. You've ruined lives, Janie Gross, and God forgive me, I helped you." Bess shook her head. "When you were little, you were so quiet, but I always knew there was something about you. Your poor mother couldn't handle you."

"You leave that witch out of this! You don't know anything."

"I know you were only five years old when they took you away from her. I know what a heartbroken little girl you were the first time I saw you. I tried to be a mother to you, but there was something that never connected inside you. Something that keeps you from understanding other people's pain. I think you lost that when you lost your mother. Or maybe you never had it."

Janie pulled the gun out of her pocket, her eyes hazed over with memories and visions from the past. "Shut up! Shut up or I'll shoot you now!" Her head hammered with pain. "I hate that woman. She's all alone now, a dried-up alcoholic who loved the bottle more than her own child. She can die for all I care."

Janie rubbed her temple with the heel of the hand holding the gun.

"I know she hurt you."

"I said shut up! Do you want to know what hurt is? Hurt is a young mother turning around and finding her baby gone. Hurt is a pathetic father standing in front of cameras begging me to give his baby back. *Me!* I'm the only one who can do that." She smiled. "They're like puppets. I pull one string, they're devastated. I pull another, they're happy and hopeful." She pointed the gun at Bess again. "Now tell me where the Loveless kid is or I'll shoot you and *you'll* know what hurt is."

"You will never find this baby. You won't get the satisfaction of watching Sunny Loveless beg and cry on national television."

"You want to know what will satisfy me?" Janie screeched, clicking the safety off the gun. "Watching *your* daughter when she finds out what you did."

Bess's eyes widened slightly. "My daughter will be just fine. She knows everything."

Janie's brain was awhirl. It was hard to think with the incessant pounding in her head.

Where was the kid? Janie didn't think the Loveless woman had it. She wouldn't have left Bess here to face Janie alone. So what had Bess done with it?

Mia. Bess's daughter.

Janie took a step forward. "Oh, really? Mia knows she was stolen fifteen years ago? Your daughter knows she has a real family out there somewhere?"

Bess blinked and her faded eyes filled with tears.

"You're lying. Mia doesn't know anything. You stupid old woman. You gave the baby to Mia." Janie laughed. "Did you think I wouldn't figure it out? I'm sure Mia will be happy to hand over the kid once she learns the truth about her *mother*."

Bess scowled. "Leave Mia out of this. She has nothing to do with it."

Janie aimed the gun at Bess. "Oh she's got a *lot* to do with it if she has the kid."

Bess shook her head.

"Where is she?" She gestured toward Bess's phone. "Wasn't she looking for an apartment near the university? Call her right now and tell her we're coming to get that kid."

"No."

"Call her or I swear I will shoot you."

"Janie, you've got to stop. The police are coming. It's over."

Bess was lying. Janie could see it in her eyes. The old woman was worse than Eddie. Why did people find it so hard to lie?

She glanced around quickly, gun still trained on Bess, and spotted a cell phone lying on the coffee table.

"If you won't call Mia, I will." She edged toward the phone. "I'm sure you've got her number in here." Picking up the cell phone, she glanced down at the display.

During that fraction of a second when her eyes were off Bess, the old woman rushed her, gnarled hands stretched out to push her off balance against the coffee table.

Janie whirled and the gun fired. The recoil knocked it out of her hand.

Bess looked startled, then her eyes rolled back and she crumpled over the coffee table, blood everywhere.

Janie stared down at her for several seconds, but she didn't move.

"Get up, you old hag! I know you're okay." She nudged her.

Nothing.

"Bess!" Damn, she was so still.

Janie felt her wattled neck. Her skin was still warm. That was good. But Janie's trembling fingers couldn't find a pulse.

Oh dear God, she'd killed her!

And she'd fallen on the cell phone. Janie cursed. Swallowing hard against the bile that rose in her throat, Janie forced herself to slide her hand under Bess's body and feel for the phone.

Warm, slick blood coated her fingers and wrist. There was so much of it!

Shuddering, swallowing acrid saliva, Janie finally touched the cool metal case. She jerked her hand back.

"Ugh!" The phone was black with blood. Backing away from her old nanny's body, Janie rushed into the kitchen and grabbed a dish towel. She scrubbed blood off her hand, then wiped the phone in it. But blood still stained her fingernails. She turned her palm up. Her life line and heart line were painted with the deep red stuff.

Forcing herself to stop staring at the blood, Janie wrapped the towel around the cell phone, then looked up at Bess's clock. She had to get out of here before anyone showed up. She started toward the back door.

The gun!

"Think, Janie. Don't get rattled." She needed a cigarette—bad. But that would have to wait. Hurrying back into the living room, she averted her eyes from Bess's body.

Where the hell was the gun?

Closing her eyes, she thought about where she and Bess had been standing. The gun had to be somewhere near the coffee table.

Sharp pains arrowed through Janie's head. Her hands were shaking as she bent over to search under the table and the couch.

There it was, on the other side of the couch. She walked around and picked it up, then ran for the back door. She used the towel to turn the knob.

As she climbed into her car, she heard traffic on the street in front of Bess's house. Was it the police?

She tossed the bloody towel and the gun into the passenger seat and started the car. She pulled out onto the street behind Bess's house, her limbs twitching with panic.

As she sped away and turned right onto McCarthy Avenue, parallel to Bergen, she licked her lips and shook her head to rid herself of the fear that strangled her. In all her years of brokering babies, she'd never made a mistake. But she'd misjudged Bess this time.

She couldn't believe Bess would do anything that would jeopardize her relationship with Mia. Janie had always counted on that. It was why she'd given her first stolen child to Bess.

She'd have bet money—she *had* bet her and Ed's future—that Bess would die before taking a chance on losing Mia.

Bess had died.

Janie practically gagged at the memory of Bess crumpled over the coffee table, blood spilling out around her.

Blood. Pumping. Blood didn't pump out of a dead body.

Janie slammed on the brakes, about a hundred yards from Oak Grove Boulevard, the main street through the town. A car rushed past.

Janie froze, but the vehicle continued on.

Glancing in her side and rearview mirrors, Janie slowed and pulled into an empty driveway. Hopefully the owners of the house were at church. Leaving her car running, she glanced around again. The little street seemed deserted.

She quickly crossed the backyard and stepped into the common area. Trees and leafy undergrowth gave her cover as she maneuvered so she could see the front door of Bess's house. She measured the distance across the yard of Bess's big old farmhouse set back from the road. She was too far away to chance running across Bess's manicured lawn.

Maybe she should drive back around. Did she have time?

As if in answer to her question, a car turned in to Bess's driveway.

Pain hammered in Janie's head.

What if Bess wasn't dead?

IT HAD TAKEN forty minutes to get to the small town of Oak Grove, east of Philadelphia.

Sunny acknowledged the wisdom of Griff's decision not to call the woman.

"I understand that she might panic and run," she told him. "I also know you're afraid this might be a trap."

"Her name is Bess Raymond," he said as he turned onto Bergen Avenue. "She's run a small day care center out of her home for over thirty years. She has one daughter, Mia, seventeen years old."

"Day care center? That explains why she has Emily. She must be keeping her for the kidnapper." Her voice was tight with desperation and hope.

He didn't answer.

"You don't think she has Emily, do you?"

"I don't know. I think she knows where Emily is. My guess is that she's involved in a baby-selling ring. Think about it. A single woman, living in a relatively isolated area, running a day care center. She's the perfect person to hold the children while arrangements are made for an illegal adoption."

"All the children who are never found." Sunny's voice tore at his sore heart.

"Right." His voice grated. Not all the children,

but many. He thought of his own little sister, with her big violet eyes and thick, dark lashes. He'd lived his entire life hoping she was alive and happy, being cared for by loving parents. The alternative was too dreadful to bear thinking of.

"Griff? You look awful. Are you all right?"

He blinked and kept his eyes on the road. "Sure. There's Bess Raymond's house."

He pulled out his cell phone and dialed one of the numbers he'd programmed into it less than an hour ago. A woman answered.

"This is Griffin Stone, FBI. Captain Sparks please."

"What are you doing?" Sunny asked.

"Alerting the locals. I told my boss I wouldn't go in without backup."

"But she might run."

He held up a hand when he heard a voice say, "Sparks, here."

"Yes, Captain Sparks. Sorry to bother you at home. That's right. My boss, Mitch Decker, called you? Good. We're approaching the Raymond woman's house now. I'd appreciate some backup in case of a problem."

"They're on standby. Shouldn't be but a couple of minutes. What about an ambulance?"

Griff looked at Sunny. If anything happened to her baby— "Yeah. If you can spare it. And

Captain, no sirens until we know what's going on, okay?"

Sparks agreed.

He disconnected and stuck the phone back into his pocket.

"How long do we have to wait?"

"Just a few minutes." He slowed down in front of the house. It was the only one on the short street. The way the area was laid out, it appeared that Bess Raymond's house had been built before the streets around her sprang up.

Sunny put a hand over her mouth and stared out the car window.

It looked quiet enough. A medium-size house with a red roof and a large, welcoming front porch. White rocking chairs were lined up close to the porch rail. The yard looked like a toddler's paradise. A slide, two swing sets and a wading pool were grouped together on one side of the long sidewalk. Colorful flower beds lined the front of the house.

Before Griff even stopped the car, Sunny grabbed the door handle.

"Wait! Damn it!" He slammed his foot on the brake and simultaneously reached across her, stopping the door from opening. "What the hell are you doing?"

She strained against his hand. "My daughter could be in that house."

"We don't know who else is in there."

Her eyes met his. Finally she stopped fighting. Her lips formed a thin line, the tendons in her neck stood out.

"We agreed to wait for backup. You have to promise me you won't do anything foolish."

She lifted her chin.

"Sunny, you have to listen to me. What good is it going to do Emily if you get yourself hurt?"

Finally her gaze faltered.

"If you'll stay here, I'll go in."

She stiffened. "By yourself?"

"Backup will be here in a couple of minutes. But you have to promise to stay in this car and out of our way."

He suffered her scrutiny as she decided whether she could trust him with the life of her child. Somehow, he passed her test. He wondered if he'd still pass if she knew about his sister.

She nodded. "Please be careful. She's just a baby."

He brought her hand to his lips. "I promise."

As Griff got out of the car, he noticed something that froze his heart. The front door was ajar.

He shot a quick glance back at the car, just enough to be sure Sunny had stayed put. She sat in the passenger seat, watching his every move.

He drew his gun. His gaze quickly assessed the

condition of the porch and the door. Nothing had been disturbed. The door didn't seem to have been forced. With his back against the wall, he glanced around the yard and the driveway, then slowly, with his gun hand, eased the door inward a fraction of an inch.

He heard a sound—a moan, coming from inside the house. *Someone was hurt!*

Clutching his gun in both hands, he shouted, "FBI. Coming in!" He shoved the door open with his shoulder and trained his gun on all corners of the dimly lit room.

Another pained moan sounded, along with labored breathing. He saw a body crumpled over the large glass coffee table.

He eased over and nudged the woman's shoulder with his gun barrel.

She sucked in a sharp breath.

"Anyone else here?" he whispered.

She didn't answer.

He checked the perimeter of the room, then quickly checked the rest of the house, acutely aware of every sound, every flicker of light.

Retracing his steps, he bent over the woman, who lay in a widening pool of blood. As he crouched beside her, he saw what lay next to her.

Griff's heart shattered, and a sob shuddered through his chest. Automatically he reached into his pocket for the handkerchief he always carried, and picked up the rattle. It was spattered with blood, but the engraving wasn't obscured.

Emily.

Ah God, not this time. Don't let me be too late this time.

He felt the woman's neck. A faint, thready pulse beat there. She was alive, at least for now. But she'd lost so much blood.

"Ms. Raymond? Bess Raymond? Can you hear me?"

A breathy moan answered him.

"Who did this? Where's the baby?"

She said something he couldn't understand, then slumped, unconscious. At the same time, Griff heard the sound of tires on gravel.

Rising, he whirled toward the door and stuck his head out, spotting the police cars and ambulance.

"Get the EMTs in here," he yelled. "She's alive!"

The ambulance drove right up to the door, destroying flower beds and leaving huge furrows in the well-kept yard.

He hurried down the steps to the car. Sunny opened the passenger door.

"Emily?" The hope in her voice struck his heart like a bullet.

"She's not in there."

"She's—not?"

She stood and grabbed his forearm with both hands. "What did Bess say? Where's my baby?"

He gently set her away from him and her gaze lit on what he held.

"Oh, God, it's hers!" She reached for the cloth-wrapped rattle.

He held it out of her reach. "I can't let you touch it, Sunny. It's evidence."

"Eviden—" Her cracked voice ripped at his soul. She pressed her lips tightly together and nodded. "I'm sorry. Of course it's evidence."

Her attention turned toward the house. "What are the EMTs doing?"

"Bess has been shot."

Sunny swayed, and he caught her shoulders, feeling them trembling. "Shot. Is she—dead?"

"No. We'll know more in a minute. Officer!" He caught the eye of a female officer, who stepped over to them immediately.

"Officer Linda Akin, sir."

Griff squeezed Sunny's shoulders. "Let Officer Akin take you to one of the police cars. You'll be safe with her."

Sunny nodded, moving stiffly. Her face was white and pinched, and her eyes were dilated. He'd seen the symptoms before. She was close to being in shock.

Griff felt the crack that she had opened inside him become a gaping chasm. If Bess Raymond died, if Sunny's daughter was never found, she would never heal. And neither would he.

But as hard as he tried to hold on to his professional distance, he knew in this instance he was not just an FBI agent. He was as invested in Sunny's daughter as she was.

"We'll find Emily, I swear on my life."

As Officer Akin led Sunny away, Griff spoke to her. "Ask the paramedics about giving her a sedative."

"I do not want a sedative!"

Griff caught the officer's eye. She nodded as she led Sunny over to the second police car.

The EMTs came out, carrying Bess Raymond on a stretcher. Griff crossed the short expanse of yard between them. He stuck the wrapped rattle into his pocket and then pulled out his badge.

"Griffin Stone, FBI." He nodded toward the stretcher. "How is she?"

The EMT in charge waved the two carrying the stretcher on into the ambulance. He peeled off his gloves.

"Small caliber gunshot wound to the chest, point-blank. Hard to believe she's still alive."

Griff's heart sank. He glanced toward the police car where the female officer had placed Sunny.

"I've got to talk to her. There's an infant missing. And this woman knows where she is."

The EMT shook his head. "She's lost too much blood, and she's got to be close to eighty years old. I doubt she'll make it to the hospital."

JANIE WATCHED IN HORROR as the ambulance pulled out onto the street, sirens blaring. She dropped her cigarette to the ground and stomped on it.

Bess was alive. *Hell and damnation.* She hadn't meant to shoot her, but damn if she didn't wish she'd killed the old hag.

Now what was she going to do? She wrapped her fingers around the weapon in her pocket as she hunkered down farther and watched the activity through the trees.

As the ambulance pulled away, Janie saw Sunny Loveless sitting alone in the backseat of the police car. A relieved sigh escaped Janie's lips as she studied her.

At least Bess hadn't been able to give her the kid.

Damn Bess, and damn Hiram. And damn Eddie, too. If they'd just come to her first, let her handle everything. But no…

Everybody had to try to think for themselves. And Janie always had to straighten everything out. Now the police were involved. Who knew what Bess had told Sunny. For all Janie knew

Hiram could have been picked up. She snorted. He was such a pansy and a coward. He'd spill his guts for a hot cup of coffee.

There was only one way to protect Eddie and her now.

She slid her gun out of her pocket and aimed it at Sunny Loveless, closing one eye.

"Bang," she whispered.

No more problem.

111 hours missing

WHEN SUNNY CAME to consciousness, she felt an all-encompassing emptiness. *Emily*. Was Emily dead?

She tried to open her eyes, but when she did the world tilted at a funny angle, so she closed them again.

Sharp, clean smells filled her nostrils, and the surface upon which she was lying was hard, but she felt the scratch of starched sheets against her arms. She was in a hospital.

Steeling herself against nausea and dizziness, she finally managed to open her eyes. When she did, she found a nurse hovering around the bed, checking an IV bag, adjusting the automatic blood pressure cuff around her arm.

She looked down. She still had on her jeans and

T-shirt but a huge needle and tubes were attached to the back of her left hand. Her gaze followed the tubes to the IV bag.

"Where am I?" she croaked. "Where's Emily?"

The nurse smiled at her. "So you're awake? You're in the Emergency Room of Oak Grove Community Hospital."

"What's wrong with me?"

"You were sedated."

Sedated. It all came flooding back. The house, the blood, Emily's rattle. The visions swirled dizzily in her head like a broken kaleidoscope.

Terror squeezed her heart. "My baby," she whispered.

The nurse looked at her oddly.

Sunny rubbed her eyes and concentrated. What had happened?

The policewoman had sat with her in the backseat of the police car until Griff had come over with one of the EMTs.

She remembered pleading with Griff not to let them sedate her, but he hadn't listened.

Once the injection took effect, everything else was a blur. She remembered being carried. Snatches of conversation floated just out of reach of her rational brain.

At one point, she'd heard one of the EMTs say something about the woman's heart.

Sunny forced herself to speak. "A woman was brought here in the ambulance with me," she whispered hoarsely to the nurse. She licked her dry lips. "I have to see her. I have to get up." She lifted her left hand and the tubing pulled, sending a burning pain through the back of her hand.

"Why do I have an IV?"

"The doctor ordered it. You were dehydrated."

"Take it out. I have to see Bess."

"Not right now."

"Please."

The nurse gently but firmly caught her hand and laid it down on the bed, then straightened the IV tubing. "You need to stay still. I'll check on her for you. Do you know her name?"

Sunny's hazy brain wouldn't work. "I don't— wait. Bess, I think. Bess something."

"I'll be back."

"Please hurry. She knows where my baby is."

GRIFF STEPPED into the curtained cubicle. Sunny's eyes were closed, her brow had that tiny frown line in the middle of it.

After the ambulance had taken off, sirens screaming, he'd spent hours with the local police as they went over Bess Raymond's house, taking fingerprints, tire prints, blood samples. He'd watched with dread as the CSU team took swab after swab after swab of blood from the living room. He prayed none of it was Emily's.

Then he'd given Captain Sparks an abbreviated version of what he'd found when he'd arrived at the scene.

As soon as he could get away, he'd come straight here. He'd tried to talk to Bess Raymond. No luck there. The gunshot had miraculously missed her vital organs. It had nicked one kidney and then exited intact.

But she was on a blood thinner after a heart attack almost a year ago, which accounted for all the blood, and made her recovery uncertain.

If Bess died, they might never find Sunny's baby. How could he bear to tell her? He reached over and ran his thumb along the tiny line between her brows, smoothing it out. Then he combed her silky hair back from her face with his fingers.

She opened her eyes.

"Griff," she said softly.

"Hi Sunny." He threw up a smiling mask to hide his worry. "Looks like you had a nice nap."

She sent him a feeble glare. "You let them drug me."

"You were about to go over the edge." He eyed the IV pole. "Looks like it was a good idea."

Her gaze sharpened. "Did you talk to Bess? What did you find out about Emily?"

"Bess lost a lot of blood."

Sunny threw back the covers and tried to struggle up, but she was blocked by the metal guardrails on the side of the hospital bed. "I want to talk to her."

"Sunny, you can't now."

Sunny's face grew pale. "Is she dead?"

"Bess Raymond has a heart condition. They had to take her right into surgery to repair the bullet wound. She's in Intensive Care on a ventilator. We haven't been able to talk to her yet."

Sunny's eyes widened with dread.

"They're trying to stabilize her. They hope she'll regain consciousness soon."

"And Emily?"

"The crime scene investigation unit is going over the house now. We found an empty infant carrier seat in the bedroom. It's being checked for trace evidence now."

"Emily's gone? They took her." Sunny put both hands over her mouth as a strangled sob escaped.

Griff stood there helplessly. He didn't know how to comfort her. All his training, all his experience, hadn't prepared him for what he was feeling now.

Each missing person was important. Each case he'd handled, he'd given everything he had. But this time, everything he had wasn't enough.

Looking at Sunny's pale face and bowed shoulders, he realized a terrifying truth. The truth that had been eating at his insides for five days. He was falling in love with her.

No. The word reverberated inside his brain, mocking him. No! His mixed-up feelings were the result of taking this case so soon after the Senator's son's death, combined with returning to Nashville. That was all.

Even as the thoughts coalesced, he knew he was lying to himself. He cleared his throat. "I'll check with the nurse about letting you leave, and we'll go get something to eat."

Sunny shook her head, dislodging tears from her eyes to slide down her cheeks. "I can't eat. I want to wait here. I have to be here when Bess wakes up. She's my only link to my daughter."

Chapter Nine

Janie glanced at the dashboard clock as she pulled into the parking lot of Oak Grove Community Hospital. She didn't have long. She had to be back home by six or six-thirty at the latest, to dress for a dinner being given by the mayor of New Rochelle in Eddie's honor. Both the lawyer and the campaign manager had recommended that they act as if nothing had happened.

She'd be cutting it close, but she'd make it. It wouldn't take her long to get ready. No one ever really looked at her anyway. They were interested in Eddie, and that was how she liked it.

She got out of the car and adjusted her baggy jacket so the .22 in her pocket wasn't weighting down the material. As she walked toward the front entrance, she quickly assessed the area. No metal detectors, no security checkpoints for visitors.

She entered and stepped up to the information desk.

The white-haired woman in a blue volunteer jacket was talking to a middle-aged man. When the man left, the woman picked up the phone and began to dial. Janie stepped directly in front of her.

The woman started, then hung up the phone. "I'm sorry," she said with a smile. "I didn't see you. May I help you?"

"Bess Raymond's room, please."

The woman nodded and consulted a computer. "Raymond...Raymond."

Janie slid her hand into her pocket and fingered the cold metal of the gun.

Try the Rs you idiot. She bit her tongue, working to keep a serene expression on her face.

"We have an Elizabeth Raymond."

"Yes. That's her. She's my aunt."

"Oh, of course. She was scheduled for emergency surgery at two o'clock. I can direct you to the surgery waiting room on the third floor. That way Ms. Raymond's doctor can reach you."

"So she didn't say anything?"

The woman frowned slightly.

"Never mind. What about Sunny Loveless?"

"Who?"

"Sunny Loveless. Another patient." Janie's fingers tightened around the handle of the gun. She'd seen the EMT give Loveless an injection and load her into the ambulance alongside Bess.

"Oh." The woman typed, then peered at the computer screen, then typed some more, then peered again. "I don't show a Loveless."

"Are you spelling it right?" Janie spoke through a clenched jaw. "It's L-O-V-E-L-E-S-S."

"I'm sorry. No one by that name has been admitted. You might check the emergency room."

"How do I get to the emergency room?"

"Follow the circular drive to the west side. Or you could walk through. This hallway leads to the employee entrance. One of the nurses might let you in."

Janie forced a smile. "Thank you." *You incompetent old relic.* She turned on her heel and left.

So Bess had made it, so far. If she was in surgery, she wouldn't be talking for a while. The question was, what had she already told Loveless?

Janie looked toward the sign that read EMERGENCY ENTRANCE. She sighed. It was getting late. She didn't have time to check on the Loveless woman.

Anger sent a streak of pain through her temple. If that ridiculous volunteer had taken any longer, Janie was afraid she might have shot her, right there in the hospital lobby.

Now, because of her, Janie had to hurry back to New Rochelle. She didn't have much time.

She'd have to come back later.

GRIFF BOOKED a double room at a hotel near the hospital. He didn't want to leave Sunny alone, for a number of reasons, not the least of which was he couldn't be sure what she'd do.

She had insisted she wasn't hungry, but he'd ordered in room service anyway. She'd sat on her bed cross-legged, and eaten a little bit of her turkey wrap, more than he'd figured she would. She'd drunk a cup of coffee, but it hadn't seemed to make much difference.

She was still drowsy from the sedative. When he saw her eyelids droop and the coffee cup tilt in her fingers, he leaned over and took the tray. Then he turned off the light on her side of the room.

"I'm not going to sleep."

He chuckled silently. "I know."

"Griff?"

"I'm right here."

"Call the hospital."

He sent her a wry smile. "I just called a half hour ago."

"Call again, please? And check with the police, to see if they've found anything?"

He took out his cell phone. "Both the hospital and Captain Sparks have promised to call as soon as they know anything at all."

Her gaze implored him.

He sighed. "Okay, but if I do, you have to sleep. Deal?"

"I'll try."

Her eyes drifted closed. Griff doubted she'd have much trouble keeping that promise.

He checked in with the hospital, and found that Bess's condition hadn't changed. The nurse told him the same thing. She said they hoped to take her off the ventilator before morning.

Then he called Captain Sparks, apologizing for the time. After he hung up he turned to let Sunny know the meager information the CSI Team had gathered from Bess Raymond's house, but she'd fallen asleep.

He watched her for a minute, as desire stirred in him. He was getting used to the torture of being so close to her. It was a sweet pain, to want her so badly.

She looked so small, so precious, lying there. He walked over and crouched by the bed, touching the little wrinkle between her brows with his thumb.

She stirred and mumbled something.

He leaned in and kissed her parted lips.

"Griff." Her mouth moved against his, and he cursed himself for waking her.

"Go to sleep," he whispered.

She lifted one hand and laid her palm against his cheek, and kissed him, her mouth soft with drowsiness, her breath like a faint breeze against his lips. Then her hand slid down his chest and her head relaxed against the pillow.

Griff closed his eyes and rose, wincing as his jeans rubbed against the sensitized flesh of his arousal.

He wiped his face and sighed, then sat at the desk and switched on his laptop. But his gaze strayed back to Sunny. When this was all over, he'd be able to walk away.

It'll be enough to see her reunited with Emily, he told himself.

Liar.

128 hours missing

SUNNY AWOKE CURLED into a fetal position, all scrunched up, with her hands fisted. She stretched. Her shoulders ached, her legs and hips were cramped and hurting.

And as soon as she came fully awake, her insides echoed with emptiness and her chest throbbed with pain. *Emily.* Emily was still gone.

The faint sound of the shower came from the bathroom and through the heavy hotel curtains, she saw a sliver of morning light. Stretching her cramped muscles with a groan, she sat up. Where was she?

The last thing she remembered was the soft brush of Griff's mouth against hers.

Slowly, the events of the last hours came back to her. She rubbed her burning eyes. She was in a hotel with Griffin Stone. She'd slept all night, thanks to the damn sedative he'd forced on her.

Sedative! Her daughter was missing, and she'd slept through the night. Anger at herself and Griff washed over her like scalding hot water. She had to get up, get dressed. Do something.

She turned over. Judging by the pristine neatness of the bedclothes beside her, Griff hadn't slept there. The other double bed was unwrinkled, too. Had he stayed up all night?

She glanced around, looking for her suitcase, and her gaze lit on Griff's laptop. It was turned away from her but she could see the flickering glow from the monitor.

She climbed out of bed and walked around the desk. On the screen was a really nice photo of a dog catching a Frisbee. As she watched, it faded out and a classic photo of the Parthenon in Centennial Park in Nashville appeared.

Fascinated, Sunny sat down. The next photograph was a close-up of a laughing toddler with dark hair and eyes the color of Griff's.

Sunny studied the photo. Was that Griff when he was little? Sunny shook her head. No, the child's clothes, and a tiny pink bow in her thick, dark hair proclaimed that she was a girl. His sister?

She didn't know if he had any family. She didn't really know anything about him, except that he was good at his job, and somehow he understood her pain. And he was a very generous lover.

The photograph changed again, and this time, the photographer had shot the little girl from about ten feet away. She was eating cotton candy and grinning. Several onlookers were watching her.

Sunny leaned in, studying the photo, trying to get a better look at the people. Something about it was odd.

The photograph began to fade. She touched the mouse, hoping to stop the photo from disappearing.

Immediately, she realized her mistake. She'd been watching the screen saver. The picture was gone.

Now she was staring at the last file Griff had been working on. It was his database of missing children.

But it wasn't open to page one, where his newest cases were listed. It was on the last page. Her heart beating with anticipation, she scanned the earliest entries.

In the bathroom, the shower cut off. She

glanced briefly toward the closed bathroom door and pushed the chair back. He'd asked her not to look at his files.

But her eyes were drawn to the screen. To the oldest entry.

It was June 30, 1991. Fifteen years ago. The date was familiar.

Her eyes scanned the fields. Date of disappearance, city, state, abductee's name and age—

"Oh, no," she whispered. "Oh, Griff…"

He'd told her this was just a job to him. But she'd known from the first day that he was lying.

Now, five days later, she knew why. It had never been just a job.

I can't do this anymore, he'd told his boss. The pain in those words had cut her. He'd told her he was an expert in missing children cases. He cared deeply about the people he helped, but he was quitting.

He was giving up.

The bathroom door opened and he emerged, bringing a puff of hot, humid air with him. He wore nothing but jeans. His bare chest and arms were sprinkled with crystalline water droplets, and he'd slung his towel around his neck.

But not even his sexy, half-naked presence could keep her attention away from what she'd just read. She dragged her eyes away from his lean waist, his taut, muscled abs, his broad shoulders, and stared at the name written next to the oldest date in his database.

Marianne Stone. Eighteen months old. Unsolved.

"What are you doing?" He stalked over to the desk and slammed the laptop closed.

He loomed over her, close enough that she could feel the damp heat that wafted from his skin, smell the faintly perfumed soap he'd showered with, and the herbal scent of his shampoo.

Close enough that she could feel his agitation.

"I told you not to look at my files."

Sunny looked up at him. "Marianne was your sister?"

His head jerked, his gaze met hers, and for an instant, Sunny saw how deep his pain went. She saw all the way down to his soul.

He whipped the towel off his neck and threw it as hard as he could toward the bathroom, cursing under his breath. Then he rounded on her.

"Why couldn't you leave it alone?" His voice was choked with emotion. "It has nothing to do with your case."

Sunny stood, a little frightened by his vehemence, her heart breaking at the grief etched on his face. "That's her in the pictures, isn't it? She was beautiful." Her eyes filled with tears.

He turned pale, started to say something, then

stopped. He sent her a slight negative shake of his head.

"What happened to her?"

"You read the entry." His voice was brittle.

She nodded. *"Unsolved."* She put her hand over her mouth to muffle a quiet sob.

"What's the matter, Sunny? Afraid I'm not capable of finding Emily?"

"What? No, of course not."

"You asked about the Senator's son the first day we met. My guess is suddenly you're having serious doubts about my ability."

Each word was a dagger, piercing her heart. His back was straight, his head held high, but Sunny saw through his indignation. She saw for the first time what he was afraid of.

He doubted his ability.

She shook her head. "I believe you can find Emily. I have to."

"Then what the hell difference does it make what happened fifteen years ago? Or last month? Why is it so important to you?"

Tears clogged her throat. "It's important to me because it's important to you. Because it's part of you. Please tell me about her."

He stood, still as a stone, and spoke in a quiet, even voice. "She was a year and a half old. I was fourteen—old enough to be responsible for my little sister. But I was more interested in my new camera. I was taking pictures, and when I turned around, her stroller was empty."

Sunny gasped. "The pictures on your screen saver—they're from the day she disappeared."

He nodded, his shoulders bowed.

"Fifteen years." Her imagination jumped fifteen years into the future, to a world without Emily. A world where she woke up every morning and asked herself whether there was something she could have done. Whether she could live another day without her baby.

"Oh, my God, Griff. How can you bear it?"

The look on his face gave her the answer. He couldn't, and yet he did. Each day of the past fifteen years was carved into the granitelike harshness of his jaw.

She looked at his laptop, then back at him. "That's how," she whispered. "That's why you do this."

"Get dressed, Sunny. We need to talk to the Crime Scene unit, and check on Bess Raymond." He grabbed a T-shirt and pulled it over his head.

"No. I want to see those pictures."

"I thought you wanted to find Emily," he threw at her.

She lifted her chin. "I saw something in one of them. It's important."

Griff ran his hands down the T-shirt to smooth it before tucking it into the waistband of his jeans. He was a little surprised to find that he still had skin.

Sunny had flayed him wide open with her questions and insights. And now she wanted to see his photographs? His private failure? He'd never shown anyone as much as she'd dug out of him in these past five days.

"No."

"Griff, please. I need to see it again. I may have—recognized someone."

"Recognized someone? Who?" He studied her keenly. What was she up to? Her number-one priority was finding her daughter. Why did she suddenly want to delay to look at his photos?

Her gaze was sharp, earnest, determined. She wasn't lying. But what was she talking about? He glanced at his watch. Seven thirty.

"Those photos were taken fifteen years ago, in Centennial Park on a Sunday. It's entirely possible that someone you knew might have been there, and gotten into one of the pictures."

"That's not it." She took a deep breath and shook her head. "I can't explain it. But I have to look again."

She looked up at him with those trusting, sad green eyes. "It has something to do with Emily, I'm sure of it."

Griff sat at the desk and opened the laptop. He accessed the graphics files where his photographs were stored. He had to steel himself to look at the file names.

Sunny read them. "*Marianne, Parthenon, dog with Frisbee, Marianne stroller*—that one. Try *Marianne stroller.*"

Griff opened the file. "That's the very last photo I took of Marianne." Never-shed tears roughened his voice.

Sunny laid her hand on his arm and the gentle understanding of her touch almost undid him. He clenched his jaw and concentrated all his strength on remaining detached.

"I turned around and saw the dog chasing the Frisbee. I moved a few steps away, sighting through the camera lens to catch the best shot. When I turned back, Marianne's—" he had to stop and clear his throat "—Marianne's stroller was lying on its side and she was gone."

His eyes devoured the pretty round face, with the dark, dark lashes and deep violet eyes that were so much like his own. "She was so beautiful," he whispered.

"I'm sorry."

He wiped his eyes, trying to make it an offhand gesture. Sunny's fingers tightened on his arm, so he doubted he'd pulled it off.

"Yeah. Me, too. So what did you see in the photo?" He shifted and straightened.

Sunny let go of his arm. She leaned in, studying the people in the photo. "Can you zoom in?"

"Sure. Here's the zoom. Go ahead." He stood. "I'm going to call the hospital, see if Bess has woken up."

Sunny sat back and looked at the entire photograph as Griff keyed in the hospital's number. She'd noticed something as the photo had appeared and disappeared on the screen saver. But looking at it now, she couldn't identify anything in particular that was odd or noticeable.

It was a pleasant photo of a pleasant afternoon in the park. The replica of the Parthenon filled the background. Couples sat on the steps, arms intertwined, heads close together. People milled about, either alone or with others.

On the other side of the room, she heard Griff asking about Bess. From his tone, it sounded as though she hadn't regained consciousness.

Sunny glanced at him. He met her gaze and shook his head. What if Bess never woke up? She was the only one who knew where Emily was.

The anguish of the empty years ahead nearly crushed her soul. She had to find Emily. *She would.*

She turned her attention back to the photo. There was *something* important in this picture. She was sure of it. She just had to find it.

A ghost of a smile played about Sunny's lips. It was no wonder that people's eyes were drawn to Marianne. She was like a dark-haired angel. A ray of sunlight caught the deep red highlights in her hair, giving the impression of a bright halo. It was a beautiful picture of a beautiful little girl.

Griff spoke. It sounded as if he was talking to the local police.

With one ear tuned to anything he might say about Emily, she concentrated on the people whose gazes seemed to be trained on Griff's sister. She zoomed in on each of them in turn.

There was nothing unusual about any of them. They were just normal people. Unremarkable. She rolled the mouse wheel, studying a man whose gaze seemed to rest on Marianne. His body language suggested that he was more interested in the young woman whose hand he held than in a baby.

Sunny moved the mouse, panning the background. A young mother holding her child looked over her shoulder toward Marianne as she walked away.

Sunny skipped over a nondescript woman who

stood alone, pushing her hair out of her eyes, and continued panning the scene. She zoomed out to look at the whole photo again.

Her eyes went back to the woman standing alone. There was nothing familiar about her, and yet... She zoomed in until the woman's head and shoulders filled the screen.

Her gaze froze on the woman's hand. All the horror of that night came back to her. The taste of leather, the empty fingers of the glove brushing her chin. Nausea twisted her gut.

"Griff!" she choked.

He held up a hand. "Right. Yes. If you'll call the hospital. We'll be there within the hour." He disconnected. "Sunny, we need to go—"

"Griff! Look at this." Sunny could barely breathe. Her pulse echoed in her head like a bass drum.

"Look at this woman." She got up. "Don't move the mouse," she cautioned as he sat down in front of the laptop.

"Look at her left hand."

"Yeah?"

"Is she missing two fingers?"

Griff zoomed in until the woman's pixilated hand filled the screen, then backed out step by step. He squinted. "It's possible. Why?"

Fear and hope collided inside her chest. "I

didn't say anything before. I wasn't sure. And I was so scared."

"Say anything about what?"

Sunny swallowed. "About the kidnapper's hand."

Griff's gaze snapped to hers. "His hand?"

She nodded. "The kidnapper had on leather gloves. And when he stuffed the note into my mouth, his hand felt odd." She took a long breath. "Like a finger of the glove, or maybe two fingers—were empty." She held up her hand, fingers spread, then curved the last two fingers in toward her palm.

"Empty?" Griff stared at her hand. "Why didn't you mention this before?"

"I wasn't sure. And then everything happened—" Her breath caught on a sob. "Griff, do you think that woman could be the kidnapper?" The horrible certainty that had been growing inside her bloomed. "Do you think she took Marianne?"

Sunny's words stabbed him. He stared at the photo. *Missing fingers.*

"Hold on." Tension scraped his throat as he switched to his database. He scrolled downward, searching for a particular entry.

"Here it is. There was a case, back in '98. A ten-month-old boy disappeared from a playpen in the green area of an apartment building in Missouri. Another mother reported noticing a slightly built brown-haired woman with a missing finger in the area."

"I was working with Violent Crimes at that time, but I read up on the case. I think the witness worked with a sketch artist, but her description was too vague, except for the missing finger."

"That has to be her!" Sunny's voice was filled with hope.

A hope that broke his heart. He'd been where she was now. Time and time again. Certain each lead was the one that would reunite him with his sister.

He shook his head, not meeting her gaze. "Don't get your hopes up, Sunny. It's a long shot. These photos are fifteen years old. I can't tell for sure that the woman's fingers are missing. It could just be the angle of her hand. In fifteen years, there's only been one case with that description."

"Two."

"All right. Two. If we count your sudden memory of the empty glove."

She glared at him. "It wasn't sudden. I just—" Her throat moved as she swallowed, and her eyes suddenly swam with tears. "I didn't mention it that night because of the note."

Griff opened his mouth to reprimand her for holding back information, but her wide sad eyes and determined chin stopped him. She'd been trying to protect her baby in the only way she knew how.

He sat down and pulled up his e-mail program. "I'll send the photo to a friend of mine, a forensic photo-analyst in D.C. Maybe he can tell us something about the woman. I'll ask him to look up the 1998 case, too, and compare them." It only took a few seconds to attach and send the photo. He stood.

"I'll call him on the way. We need to get going. Captain Sparks has obtained authorization for you to visit Bess Raymond in the hospital, and I need to go to the police station. They found several cigarette butts in a wooded area near her house. They think someone was watching, possibly even while the police were there."

"Do you know who?"

He shook his head and put his hands on her shoulders. "I'm going to leave you at the hospital. I'll be gone a few hours. We may go out to the crime scene. Bess has a police officer guarding her. As soon as she can talk, the officer will notify a detective to take her statement. You'll be able to see her then. Don't leave the hospital for any reason. If you stay put, you'll be perfectly safe."

132 hours missing

SUNNY PACED the short length of the intensive care waiting room. There were several other people in the room. They all had worry etched on their faces. All but the toddler who sported his mother's red hair. He sat on her lap, gaily bouncing up and down. Sunny couldn't help but smile at his innocent happiness. She'd already formed images of Emily as a toddler, already signed her up for a day care center, already started looking at the pretty ruffled dresses in the department stores.

Her empty heart's hollow beating echoed through her.

The toddler's mother met Sunny's gaze. She acknowledged her smile with a sad little smile of her own. The crumpled tissue she clutched and her red-rimmed eyes told Sunny that, so far, whoever she was there to see was not doing well.

An older woman was sitting with a couple who had probably brought her to the hospital this morning, because they all appeared freshly showered and their clothes were fresh and un-wrinkled, unlike their faces.

She looked at the clock that hung over the door. She'd been waiting for almost two hours. The brief, coveted ten o'clock visiting time had come and gone, and no one had called her. The grizzled volunteer sitting at the information desk had given her a message when she arrived. Bess Raymond had regained consciousness and was being taken off the ventilator.

Sunny stopped in front of the desk.

"Can you check with the nurses' station again? If she's awake, I don't understand what the delay is."

The man stopped checking the list of names before him and looked up. The shapeless blue jacket that identified hospital volunteers contrasted sharply with his weathered skin. "They'd have called me."

"Are you sure? Maybe they got busy and forgot."

"The nurses know you're here. You should have a cup of coffee and sit down. Things go slow sometimes. I'll let you know." His kind expression softened his words.

Sunny tried to smile at him. "Thank you." She didn't want any coffee. She wanted to talk to Bess. Bess knew where Emily was.

She sat down in one of the chairs and tried to watch the TV that was set to a local morning show, but all she could see before her eyes was Bess lying so still in the ambulance, with blood staining her clothes, and the concerned faces of the emergency medical team.

She didn't remember much after that. She'd succumbed to the sedative and slept the rest of the way to the emergency room.

A second volunteer stepped into the room. Everyone stopped talking and turned toward her. Did she have a message for someone?

The woman stood for a few seconds, her hands in the big patch pockets of her blue jacket, then leaned over and said something to the man at the desk, who nodded in Sunny's direction.

Sunny's heart leaped as the woman started toward her. The murmur of conversation rose again as the others realized she wasn't looking for them.

Sunny stood.

"Are you Ms. Loveless?"

"Yes." Sunny's pulse raced. "Am I going to get to see Bess now?"

The woman nodded. "That would be Bess Raymond, right? She's been moved to a private room. I'll show you the way."

"Really? Already?" Sunny was surprised. "She must be doing very well." She glanced at the male volunteer, but he was still busily checking his list. Why hadn't he told her Bess was going to be moved?

"She is." The woman shouldered the door open so Sunny could exit. "Go left, down to the end of the hall and turn left again."

The volunteer waited until Sunny passed her. There were no patient rooms on the hall. Its doors were marked STORAGE, HOUSEKEEPING CLOSET, LINENS.

"The elevators are about halfway down."

Sunny peered down the hall. "I thought the elevators were on the front side of the hospital."

"These are the service elevators. They're quicker. We're going to the first floor."

Sunny frowned as she stepped into the elevator. "First? There aren't any patient rooms down there, are there?"

The woman stepped inside and stood beside her, sending her a bland smile. "This is a shortcut. Ms. Raymond was moved to the new wing. To get there, we have to go to the lobby and take a different set of elevators."

Sunny pressed the button marked 1.

"I'm so glad my—friend is doing better. I've been worried."

"We all have."

Sunny frowned at the woman. That was an odd thing to say. Her scalp tingled. "Do you know Bess Raymond?"

The woman smiled. "Of course. She raised me."

The little sign in Bess's front yard and the children's toys and playground. "You were in her day care center. She's good with children?"

"The best." The woman coughed.

"Here we are," she said as the elevator doors opened. "I just need to check in with my supervisor for a moment."

Anxious and impatient, Sunny waited while the woman stepped over to the front desk and asked to use the phone. She made a quick call, then hung up.

She glanced around the lobby, then returned to Sunny's side.

"Which way is the new wing?" Sunny asked.

"Listen to me." The woman stepped up close behind Sunny and thrust something hard into the middle of her back.

A gun. Sunny gasped and froze. "What—"

"Shut up. Go straight down this hall and out the end door. A taxi will be here to pick us up in a couple of minutes.

The gun dug into the sensitive flesh between Sunny's ribs. She could barely breathe, her chest was so tight with fear. "What are you doing? Do you have Emily—?"

"I said shut up." The woman coughed. "You make the slightest move to get away or alert anyone and I will shoot you in the back."

Sunny swallowed the scream that pushed at her throat. There was a note of confidence in the woman's voice. She meant what she said.

"Do you believe me?"

Sunny nodded. "Y-yes. You shot Bess, didn't you?"

"Keep moving."

Sunny glanced at a young man in green scrubs who passed them going in the opposite direction. He didn't even look at them.

"Who are you?" she whispered.

The gun jabbed into her ribs. "What did Bess tell you?"

"I haven't talked to her. I was waiting. I thought you—"

"You're lying. I called over an hour ago, told them I was her cousin. They said she was awake. Now open the door."

Sunny's knees shook. Her head spun. Terror cramped her muscles. This was the woman who had shot Bess.

She pushed on the exit door. It opened into an employee parking lot. There were a lot of cars and no people. Even if Sunny had found the courage to alert someone, there was no one around.

"Walk to your right, up to the main driveway. And stop looking so damn scared."

She did as she was told.

Just as they reached the driveway, her cell phone rang.

The woman cursed, then stuck out her left hand. "Give me your damn purse."

Sunny looked down. Shock turned her heart to ice. The woman's hand was missing two fingers—the ring finger and the pinkie.

She tried to speak, but her throat wouldn't work. A sob shook her.

Finally she found her voice. "It was you. You took my baby," she choked out. She couldn't even cry. Her chest felt crushed in a vise. "Where is she? Please tell me."

The phone rang again, and again.

The woman jerked Sunny's purse out of her numb hands, and dug out the cell phone. "Shut *up!*"

After glancing around to be sure no one was watching, she dropped the phone onto the concrete pavement and stomped on it.

The metallic crunch screeched through Sunny's brain, accompanied by the crunch of tires on gravel as the taxi stopped.

"Get in! And keep your mouth shut." The woman pushed Sunny into the car and climbed in beside her.

Sunny clasped her hands in her lap and stared at the back of the taxi driver's head.

The woman gave him an address that sounded familiar. Was it Bess's street?

Think. What could she do? Should she try to fight? To run?

The cold metal of the gun barrel dug into her side. The taxi driver turned up his radio. A country station was playing something about loving and leaving.

"We're going to Bess's house?"

"Don't talk."

Had Griff said Sparks was going to take him out to the house? Sunny couldn't remember, but a glimmer of hope fluttered in her chest. "Why there?"

"Bess has something I need. And this way, I can dispose of two problems at the same time." She pressed the gun deeper into Sunny's side. "Now tell me what Bess told you."

"I haven't been able to see her yet."

"Not today. *Before,* when she called you."

Sunny tried to think like a detective. The woman had to be Jane Gross. The landlord's description fit her perfectly. There was nothing distinctive about her. She had dull brown hair, a pale face with small, unremarkable features. She was her own perfect disguise. Her description would fit a million women.

The only photos Sunny had seen of Jane were newspaper clippings of political events. It was impossible to say whether this woman was the same person that stood by Ed Gross in those blurry pictures.

But Griff's photo, and the empty fingers on

the glove told the whole story. Certainty gripped Sunny. This woman had stolen Emily. And fifteen years ago, she'd stolen Griff's sister.

She had to stifle a gasp. She was in the presence of a monster.

She turned and looked directly into Jane Gross's eyes. "If my baby is dead," she whispered, "then I don't care what you do to me." Griff's face rose in her mind, right beside her daughter's, and a suffocating grief swathed her. Tears spilled down her cheeks and she choked back a short, pained sob. But she didn't look away.

Jane ground her teeth and glanced toward the taxi driver. "Your precious kid is not dead—yet."

Sunny's hand flew to her mouth. She sucked air into her burning lungs. Her gaze searched Jane's dull eyes.

"Don't lie to me, please." Hope flared painfully inside her.

Jane rolled her eyes and bared her small teeth. "Stop sniveling or I *will* shoot you."

"Who—" Sunny swallowed her tears. She had to concentrate, had to find out everything she could, in case she was able to get away. "Who are you? You're Jane Gross, aren't you?"

"I'll tell you who I am, you stupid busybody. I'm someone you should have left alone. We Specialize in Happy Endings." Her voice was mocking. "What the hell did you think you were doing? One person's happy ending can ruin another's life."

Sunny nodded numbly. She'd been so naive, so arrogant, thinking she could dispense happiness like Valentine candy. Maybe Griff was right. Maybe there were no happy endings. "But what did I do to you?"

"You meddled in our lives. Brought up things that should have been buried forever."

"It's true. Jennifer Curry *is* your daughter."

"Shut *up!* This is all your fault. You deserve to die."

"That's what you're going to do? Kill me?"

"Probably."

The offhand answer didn't even frighten Sunny. Only one thing stabbed deep into the empty place where her heart used to be. She'd never see Emily again. A sadness too deep for tears engulfed her.

She thought about Griff, and the way he'd looked at the photographs of his sister. How had he done it? How had he maintained hope through all these years?

Griff. He'd taught her so much in the few days she'd known him. She saw his violet eyes in her mind, electrified by passion, darkened by sadness, soft and warm as he looked at her.

A sense of calm swept through her. If Jane

killed her, at least she'd had a taste of her own happy ending. She'd had Emily.

And for one moment out of time, she'd had love. Remembering the compassion and under-standing in Griff's eyes, she knew in her heart that he would make sure Emily was all right.

Suddenly, determination flowed through her. She lifted her chin. She was not ready to give up. Never. As long as she was alive.

"I need to see my baby."

"Why?" Jane's voice grated through clenched teeth. "It's not even your kid. You got it from some little whore who didn't want it."

She stared at the other woman, shocked. "Of course she's mine. I'm her mother. It's not based on biology. It's based on love."

Jane's brow furrowed for an instant. Sunny watched her. Had something she'd said gotten to her?

"You sentimental little pansy. You sound like Bess. It's based on *nothing*. Kids aren't good for anything. They're whiny and helpless and always in the way."

Jane's words came from somewhere outside of herself. They were awful, hateful, damaging words. In a flash of insight, Sunny understood. Jane had heard those words—probably from before she could talk.

"Bess didn't tell you that."

"No. Bess is a sucker for kids."

"So it was your mother."

Jane's face went red with anger. "You shut *up!* Unless you want to die right here, right now, and never see your *daughter* again."

Chapter Ten

Griff listened to the canned voice telling him the cellular customer he was trying to reach was unavailable.

"Damn it, Sunny!" He shot up out of the chair and punched Redial. A sick crawling in his gut told him something had happened to her.

Captain Sparks gathered up the photographs of cigarette butts and tire tracks. "So CSU has ID'd the tires as consistent with a late-model Lexus, and Trace is working on lifting DNA from the cigarette butts."

Only half hearing him, Griff listened to the phone ring and ring. "There's something wrong."

"Maybe she's talking to Bess Raymond. My detective is on her way over to the hospital. She'll check on her."

Griff snapped his phone shut and cursed.

"Now, son," the older man said, "the hospital's

got a rule about using cell phones inside the building."

"She'd answer." Griff rubbed his chest, where apprehension burned. "I've got to get over there."

Sparks was already on the phone. He spoke for a moment, then hung up. "The officer guarding Ms. Raymond hasn't seen her. The detective just got there."

"Tell the officer to page her. Talk to hospital personnel and families. Find out who saw her last. Tell him to ask if anybody noticed anything unusual."

Sparks nodded, a wry sympathetic amusement showing in his face. "The officer knows what to ask."

"Right. Sorry sir. I've got to go."

Griff knew he wasn't acting like an FBI agent. He didn't feel like one. He was losing it. He felt as he'd felt at fourteen—terrified, helpless and horribly afraid he had lost the one person he loved most in the world.

Aw hell. The raw burning in his chest spread out through his entire body. His hand shook as he grabbed his jacket. He had to find her. *Now.*

Lost in tormented thought, Griff followed Sparks out to his car.

He didn't want to love Sunny. He didn't want to love anybody—ever again. He'd learned too young how awful losing a loved one was.

By the time Sparks pulled into the hospital parking lot, Griff had reached a heartbreaking realization. He couldn't make himself stop loving Sunny. No more than he could forget Marianne.

It was hopeless, a love built on shared pain, shared tragedy. Griff knew that if he couldn't give Sunny back her child, there would be no happy ending for either of them.

She had needed something that night, something he'd been able to supply, at least for a while. His body stirred at the memory of her beneath him, moaning with passion, clinging to him as she took him deep inside her, as she cried out with fulfillment.

But the need to feel alive, to feel safe and cherished, wasn't enough to build a life on. Another lesson he'd learned. Using someone else to ease your pain didn't work for very long. It was why he had made up his mind long ago not to love anyone.

But now he'd even failed in that.

He loved her. He'd just have to deal with it.

Captain Sparks led the way to the intensive care unit and flashed his badge. The nurse nodded and opened the automatic door into the large circular room surrounded by glass-enclosed cubicles.

She pointed toward one of the rooms. Griff could see the detective inside.

"Has Sunny Loveless been in to see Ms. Raymond?" Griff asked.

The nurse shook her head. "The policewoman already asked about her."

Tense with worry and torn between what he wanted to do and what he needed to do, Griff thanked her and turned to Sparks.

"Captain—"

Sparks nodded. "The officer knows we're here. He'll let us know if they find her."

Fear still engulfed Griff. Sunny wasn't here. He knew it. Something had happened.

"I know you're worried about her, son. She can't have gone far."

As they stepped inside the monitored room, the young detective stood. Griff nodded at her.

The only light in the room was the blue from the monitors surrounding the bed. Bess Raymond's gray hair looked dingy against the clean white sheets. She looked small and old, her face wrinkled and pale.

A nurse was watching the monitors.

"How's she doing?" Sparks asked the detective.

"She's pretty doped up. She just barely managed to tell me her name."

"Wait outside, would you? Help the officer canvass the employees and visitors."

"Yes, sir. No problem." She left.

"Ms. Raymond?" Griff said softly.

Her thick, gnarled fingers twitched and she opened her eyes. She licked her lips. The nurse held a cup so she could sip a little water through a straw.

Griff took the cup and held it. "Ms. Raymond, can you talk?"

"Who are you?" she croaked. "Another…cop?"

"I'm an FBI Special Agent. I'm looking for Emily Rose Loveless."

"Emily Rose," Ms. Raymond mumbled. "Get her back to…her mother. Missing her."

Griff's eyes prickled. "That's right. Her mother misses her a lot. Do you know where Emily is?"

The woman's weak blue eyes cleared, and she looked straight at Griff. "Can't let Janie find her."

Griff glanced at Sparks. "Jane Gross."

Sparks nodded. Reaching into his pocket for his cell phone, he stepped out of the room. "That should be enough to get them picked up for questioning."

"Tell me, Ms. Raymond. Tell me about Janie."

The nurse took the cup of water from Griff and set it on the tray table, then left.

"Ms. Raymond?"

Bess Raymond's eyes were closed again. "Tired," she said.

"I know. You've been shot. Do you know who shot you?"

Her fingers picked at the blanket that covered

her. "Tired of helping her hide those poor babies…"

Griff's pulse pounded. "Did you say babies? Have there been others?"

Long-buried hope clawed its way up from deep within him. He resisted its pull. He'd given up hope of ever finding his sister. "Ms. Raymond. I need to know where Emily is."

"Excuse me, sir?"

The tinny voice coming through the intercom unit on the bed rail startled Griff.

"Yes? Griffin Stone here."

"Sir, there's a call for Ms. Raymond. Do you want to take it?"

"Yes!" Griff stood, just as the phone on the bedside table rang softly. He lifted the receiver.

"Bess Raymond's room."

For a few seconds, there was nothing but the sound of soft rapid breathing.

"Hello?" He spoke softly. Was it Sunny? He didn't dare ask. He didn't want to frighten whoever it was into hanging up.

"Who is this?" a young female voice asked.

It wasn't Sunny. Griff's chest tightened. He shook his head. He had to stop obsessing over her safety. The police were looking for her. His job was here. He had to find Emily.

He concentrated on the barely suppressed

panic in the girl's voice and chose his words carefully. "I'm helping Ms. Raymond. Who's this?" He held his breath.

"Is—is she all right?"

"She's resting comfortably." He took a risk. "Is this her daughter? She's been asking about you." It wasn't too much of a lie.

He heard a relieved sigh. "Can I talk to her?"

He glanced at Bess, whose eyes were closed. "She's asleep right now. Is this Mia?" he asked, remembering Natasha's information about Mrs. Raymond's daughter.

A pause. "Yes." Her voice was strangled with tears.

Griff debated whether to tell Bess's daughter who he really was. Would it reassure her or frighten her away?

"Is there anything you want me to tell your mother?" he asked.

Bess's fingers began twitching. She picked frantically at the blanket.

Griff heard something through the phone line. Not Mia's voice. It was something in the background. Was it a cry? A *baby's* cry?

Adrenaline surged through him, sucking the breath out of him with a thrill of anticipation.

"No. I should go." Her voice sounded panicked. "I just wanted to be sure—"

Another cry. It *was* a baby. *Dear God, let it be Emily.*

"Mia? Listen to me." Griff tried to control his voice. He didn't want to let on to the girl that he'd heard the baby's cry.

"I really—"

"Mia. My name is Griffin Stone. Your mother is helping us try to find a missing baby."

Mia made a distressed sound. "H-helping who?"

"Mia. I want you to listen closely. I'm an FBI Agent. I'm protecting your mother."

He heard her gasp.

"Mia, don't hang up. Mia?"

The phone went dead.

"Damn it!" He gripped the receiver in his fist, wanting to smash something with it. But with a huge effort, he relaxed his fingers and hung it up. He reached for the glass door.

"Nurse, get Captain Sparks. I need that call traced."

The nurse looked up.

"Now!" he snapped.

He glanced back at the bed. He wanted to be out there, looking for Sunny, or tracing Mia's call. But he needed information that only Bess had.

Breathing deeply to calm his racing heart, he pulled a chair up close to the bed.

"Bess, are you awake?"

Her fingers twitched. "Mia?"

"Yes, that was Mia. She called to check on you."

Bess's eyes opened. "You're FBI?"

Griff forced a smile. "So you were listening?"

"Not dead yet."

"Bess, I need to find your daughter. She has Sunny's baby, doesn't she?"

Bess closed her eyes and nodded. "Never should have—"

"It's okay. Trust me. I know you were protecting the baby. I know you called Sunny."

"I couldn't refuse to take—the baby. Janie hates babies." She licked her lips. "Babies need love."

"Yes, they do." He patted her wrinkled hand.

"The rattle?"

"We found Emily's rattle."

"Kept it to prove—"

He nodded. "To prove you were telling the truth about Emily."

She nodded weakly. Then, with a sudden surge of strength, Bess grasped his wrist. "Mia! You've got to stop her."

He leaned closer. "Stop her?"

"I told her if anything happened to me…"

Griff waited, his heart pounding.

"Told her to get the book."

"The book?"

Bess closed her eyes and sighed.

"Bess. What book?"

"Book of children. At my house. Janie wants that book."

"And Mia knows where it is?"

Bess swallowed. "Mia knows everything."

"Bess." He squeezed her hand. "Don't worry. Tell me how to reach Mia. We'll protect her."

"And the baby," Bess whispered.

He felt the sting of tears. Clenching his jaw, he nodded. "And the baby."

135 hours missing

SUNNY COULDN'T TEAR her eyes from the obscene black stain of blood on the oak coffee table. It was Bess Raymond's blood. She couldn't help but wonder if any of it was Emily's.

Jane prodded her with the gun. "Go on. I don't have all day."

She swallowed. "You shot her. Why?"

Jane laughed. "Because she didn't listen to me. After all these years, old Bess finally decided she could think for herself. Surprised the hell out of me. I didn't think she had it in her."

Sunny watched Jane in fascination. How could she have thought she was nondescript? Her brown eyes glittered with evil lights. Her face was sharp and sallow, the skin drawn across her bones as tightly as a latex glove. She moved quickly, jerkily, like a bird.

At first, Sunny had thought she was mad. But she wasn't. She was brilliant and deadly. And she had Emily.

"Where's my baby?"

"Get to work. I need that book."

Jane's cold voice sent chills through Sunny. "I don't know anything about a book."

Jane bared her teeth in a sneer. "Then you'd better get started." She looked at her watch. "I have to leave by six o'clock. Ed is appearing at a town meeting. If you haven't found the book by then, well…" She shrugged.

"What about Emily?"

"That's up to you. Find the book in time, and you might get to see your kid."

…before you die. Sunny filled in the unspoken words. They didn't have the power to frighten her anymore. She knew Jane was going to kill her.

"Swear to me that Emily is safe."

"Oh please." Jane rolled her eyes. "Your kid is fine. I'm not a monster."

Yes you are.

Monsters came in all shapes and sizes. All Sunny could do was pray that Jane was telling the truth about Emily. Hope was all she had. She'd cling to it as long as she could.

"What kind of book is it?"

"It has names. Dates," Jane said. "Like a diary."

"Where do you want me to start?"

Jane pushed her hair back in the same gesture that Griff had caught on film. "Hell if I know. Just find it."

Sunny surveyed the large living room. The police and the EMTs had made a mess. Furniture was pushed aside. Fingerprint dust coated everything. From TV, Sunny knew the paper curls were the backing of fingerprint tape.

Half of the room was set up as a children's play area. A big walnut desk nearby held a portable TV and a computer.

"Maybe the desk?"

Jane coughed and pulled out a pack of cigarettes. "Fine by me." She manipulated a lighter with her deformed left hand and took a long drag.

The smell of cigarette smoke drifted toward Sunny as she sat down in the wooden desk chair and pulled out the center drawer. The wheels on the chair squeaked as she moved.

Jane paced in front of the windows, smoking and clicking the safety of the gun on and off, on and off, *on and off*.

THE CLICK OF THE GUN'S SAFETY echoed in Sunny's head like the ticking of a clock as she searched frantically. She'd been bent over the huge desk for what felt like hours, as Jane smoked and coughed and paced. The cavernous drawers were filled with a lifetime of receipts, letters, tax records. It appeared that Bess had kept everything in the desk. Sunny had long since decided that whatever "the book" was, it wasn't in the desk. But she was afraid to stop looking.

"You don't have much time," Jane said.

But Sunny barely heard her. Her attention was on something she'd just glimpsed in the bottom of the far right drawer, behind a row of files. She bent over and reached into the depths of the drawer. Her fingers touched fine-grained leather.

Her pulse drummed in her temple. It was a pocket-size journal. *Was this the book?*

She dug out a handful of files and sat them on top of the desk, alongside a mountain of papers.

She wanted to grab the journal, shove it in Jane's face and demand to see Emily.

But Jane was a liar. As soon as she had the book, she'd kill Sunny.

"Did you hear what I said?"

Sunny composed her face before she looked over her shoulder. "Yes. This is the last drawer."

Jane dropped a cigarette and crushed it on the hardwood floor. "That's it. You're useless. Get up."

"But I'm almost done. It could be in here. Give me a few more minutes, please."

Jane lifted the gun. "I said—" She stopped and cocked her head. *She'd heard something.*

Sunny tensed, trying to hear what Jane had heard.

Was it Griff? A fierce, burning hope blossomed in her chest. She hadn't dared to believe he'd find her in time. It was hard enough sustaining the faint hope that she would see Emily again.

She'd told herself it was enough that he'd been there for her when she'd needed his strength. That he'd allowed her to use him for safety and shelter. For love.

Before she had time to explore her thought, she heard the rattle of keys. Someone was unlocking the back door.

Jane crossed the living room in two strides and flattened herself against the wall between the living room and dining room, her attention focused on the footsteps coming toward them.

Sunny bent slightly, holding her breath and praying that the chair wouldn't creak. She managed to grasp the leather journal with two fingers. She lifted it slowly, never taking her eyes off Jane. When she shifted to slide it into the pocket of her slacks, the wheels squawked loudly.

Jane turned the gun on her for an instant, a hard glint in her eyes.

The message was clear. *Stay put or you're dead.*

Sunny swallowed, then nodded.

GRIFF AND SPARKS, along with several backup black-and-whites, headed toward Bess's house.

Sparks had just hung up from talking to the New Rochelle police, and Griff was on the phone to Natasha, who had been in touch with the photo-analyst.

"Hart said he couldn't positively identify Jane Gross from your photograph," Natasha said. "But he did say he could state under oath that the facial characteristics, build and other identifying features were consistent with hers. He also said the woman in your photo does have a deformity of her left hand."

"Can you verify that Jane Gross has a similar problem?"

"Already done. We have eyewitness testimony from people who know her. And her fingerprints are on file, because of her husband's campaign."

"What about the husband?"

"He's cooperating with the New Rochelle police. He is adamant that his wife is visiting her mother in Springfield."

"Yeah?"

"Mrs. Roe is in a nursing home, paid for by her

daughter. The daughter hasn't visited her in over two years. Jane's been lying to hubby."

"What about Bess Raymond? And her daughter?"

"Right. Adopted. I found the records. The papers were drawn up by a Hiram Cogburn, and executed by a lawyer in Philadelphia. Mia Raymond was supposedly a foundling. Her birth certificate was created after the fact."

"We're almost there," Sparks said.

"Okay, Natasha. Thanks."

"Griff, Ed Gross said there's a town meeting tonight. Jane promised him she'd be there."

"What time?"

"Seven o'clock. He said she's never missed a political event. She's always by his side."

"Thanks." Griff disconnected. "We've got a problem," he told Sparks. "Jane is due back in New Rochelle by seven o'clock."

"That's a good hour and a half drive."

Griff looked at his watch and cursed. "It's five now."

Sunny. God he hoped he wasn't too late. According to Bess, the book she asked Mia to retrieve was a journal. It contained evidence of all the children Jane had stolen and brought to Bess to care for over the years.

He was gambling everything that Jane had kidnapped Sunny, and had brought her to Bess's house to find the book. If he was wrong, he'd just condemned her and her daughter to death.

"Don't approach the place directly. Park on the next street where the cigarette butts were found, and walk through the common area. If anyone is at the house I don't want to alert them."

Sparks nodded, reaching for his radio mic. He directed the backup officers to turn on Edgar Street, parallel to Bergen, and park out of sight of Bess Raymond's house.

Griff pulled out his gun and checked it, working to keep his emotions under control. He couldn't stop picturing Sunny, her eyes wide and trusting.

Please let me keep my promise this time, he prayed.

As soon as Sparks stopped the car, Griff was out.

Sparks stopped him in front of the car. "Wait for backup," he said.

Griff shook his head. "There's no time."

"Son, I'm ordering you—"

Griff leveled his gaze at the police captain. "Sorry, sir, you don't have the authority."

Sparks frowned, but said nothing more.

Griff picked his way through the trees and undergrowth until he could see Bess's house.

Was Sunny in there? Was she still alive?

SUNNY WATCHED the darkened archway that connected the living room with the dining room in horrified fascination. The light, cautious footsteps came closer and closer.

Jane had flattened her back against the shadows by the door. She shifted and a glimmer of late-afternoon sunlight flashed off the barrel of her gun.

Sunny held her breath. She wanted to cry out— to warn whoever was about to walk into Jane's trap.

Jane glanced at her then back at the door. To Sunny's surprise, she slipped the gun into the big patch pocket of her volunteer jacket.

A muffled sound reached Sunny's ears. It was a baby's cry. *It was Emily!*

All the blood drained from her head and she felt faint. Her throat clogged with tears, her heart swelled with relief and joy even as fear stole her breath.

Was this what Jane had meant when she'd tantalized Sunny with the possibility of seeing Emily again? Was this part of Jane's plan?

At that instant a teenage girl holding an infant carrier stepped through the doorway, her eyes wide with terror.

"Hello, Mia," Jane said.

The girl started and whirled. Her knuckles

went white as bones where she gripped the carrier's handles.

"Emily," Sunny croaked, trying to see the baby in the carrier.

The girl's head jerked toward her, then back to Jane. "Aunt Janie? What's going on?"

"It's all right, Mia."

"My mother's in the hospital. Someone shot her. She told me—"

Mia wasn't in on it. Relief flowed through Sunny. She had to see Emily. She rose and started toward her.

"Stop!" Jane's hand went to her pocket. "Don't move another inch."

"Who—" Mia started.

"I'm Emily's mother."

"Watch it, Loveless." Jane's eyes never left Sunny as she spoke to Mia. "Mia, honey, set the baby down."

"What are you doing, Aunt Janie?" Mia didn't move.

Sunny couldn't tear her eyes away from the carrier. She could see Emily's little arms waving, hear her familiar whimper.

Sunny knew that cry. Her daughter was hungry. Anguish and longing tore at her.

"Please," she begged.

Mia's big dark eyes met hers and although the

room was too dark to see much more than a silhouette, Sunny had an odd sense of déjà vu.

Jane looked at her watch. "Well, time's up and
I don't have the book."

"Mia," Sunny said brokenly, "take Emily outside."

"No!" Jane moved her hand in her pocket, and
Sunny knew the gun was pointed directly at her.

She swallowed her tears and straightened.
"Yes," she said, slowly sliding the leather journal
from her slacks.

Jane's eyes glittered.

"I've got your book, Jane."

"That's my mother's book." Mia started
forward. "She told me to come and get it."

"Mia, don't," Sunny cried.

Jane moved so quickly that Sunny barely
realized what she was doing. She snaked her arm
around Mia's neck and pulled the gun from her
pocket.

"Aunt—"

Jane tightened her hold.

Sunny froze. "Don't hurt them. It's me you
want." She held out the book. "Let Mia take
Emily and leave. Then you and I can…settle up."

"I don't have time for this. I have a town
meeting tonight," Jane snarled. "I'll have to

drive like hell to get back in time. Give me the damn book."

Sunny wondered if there was any reason to stall. If Mia could get Emily away without either of them being harmed, that should be enough. But somehow it wasn't.

Emily deserved a mother who was brave enough to fight for her. And God help her, Sunny didn't want to die without holding her daughter one more time, or seeing Griff.

Something tickled at the edge of her mind. Something that might have been important had she not been facing a loaded gun.

"Jane, you can have the book, as soon as you let them go." She held the journal up so it caught the sun's rays shining through the window.

Jane coughed. "Go wait for me in the other room, Mia."

Mia stared wide-eyed at Sunny.

"Go," Sunny said, hoping Mia had sense enough to keep going, right out to her car. "Take Emily and go."

Jane let go of the girl and pushed her out of the way.

Mia bent and picked up Emily's infant carrier, then disappeared through the door, her shoes clicking on the hardwood floors. Sunny's heart shattered. She swallowed a sob.

"Give it to me."

"First, tell me what I did to you."

Jane laughed, a harsh sound that ended in a cough. "I don't have time for the TV show wrap-up. Sorry. Besides, if you're too dumb to know—"

Sunny played to Jane's arrogance. "Then shoot me. But I think you have the wrong person. I've never even met you."

"How can the world be so full of stupid people? You went to see Eddie. You got him all upset about that girl."

"*That girl* is your child."

"Oh please. Now you sound like Eddie."

"Eddie wanted his daughter, didn't he?" Sunny knew she was treading on dangerous ground. But she had nothing to lose. Jane was going to kill her anyway. If she could keep her talking long enough for Mia to get Emily to safety...

"Eddie's a sentimental old fool. I'm about to make him a congressman. And now you show up and ruin everything. You already had old Mabry stirred up. He'd totally forgotten about us until you started asking your questions."

"I don't understand."

Jane rolled her eyes and took two steps forward, pointing the gun at Sunny's heart. "Mabry knew the date we left. When you mentioned the date to Eddie, I knew you'd figured it all out."

The date. Sunny tried to ignore the gun. What was so important about the date?

"June 30th," she muttered. In her mind's eye, she saw the entry in Griff's database. June 30, 1991 was the same day Griff's sister had disappeared. Then she remembered an article in the newspaper archives about a stolen child.

Oh dear God! "You stole Marianne. The toddler in Centennial Park, fifteen years ago."

"See!" Jane waved the gun. "You've figured it all out. Now you have to die."

Chapter Eleven

Griff watched as the back door opened. He trained his gun on it, his heart beating so wildly that he could hardly hold the weapon steady.

A dark-haired teenager carrying an infant carrier ran out the door toward her car. It had to be Mia.

He stepped in front of her, holstering his gun.

When she saw him she gasped and opened her mouth to scream, but he held out his badge. "Shh. I'm Griff Stone. I talked to you on the phone about your mother," he said softly, keeping an eye on the back door and his gun hand ready at his side. "Is that Emily?"

"Yes," she sobbed. "I don't understand—"

"Who's in the house?"

"Aunt Janie, and Emily's mother, I think." She wiped her eyes. "She has Mom's book."

"Get in your car and drive to McCarthy Avenue. There are police there. They'll take care of you."

The girl nodded, but she didn't move.

"Go on," he said gently.

He turned toward the door, his limbs tingling with a combination of relief and fear.

Emily was safe. *Thank God.*

But what about Sunny? Worry ate at his gut. He moved carefully toward the back door and eased it open. It was dark inside the house. He blinked and shook his head, hoping his eyes would dark-adapt quickly.

He heard voices.

Carefully, he moved through the kitchen into the dining room. The murmur of voices increased in volume. He recognized Sunny's voice, and the familiar melodic tones nearly undid him. She was all right, so far. Hot relief tightened his scalp.

Then he heard the other voice—harsh, nervous. It was *Jane*. At least she was talking.

Just as he approached the archway into the living room, the voices stopped.

He heard the creak of unoiled wheels rolling over wood.

Then a gunshot.

Oh God, no!

He rounded the doorway, weapon up, ready to fire. For a horrible instant, he couldn't see anything in the darkness. Then a shadow moved.

Both women were down!

"Sunny!" he shouted.

The figure closest to him shoved a desk chair in his direction and he saw the glint of sunlight on metal.

He dived to the floor and rolled just as a bullet whizzed past his ear. Damn it, he couldn't fire. He didn't know where Sunny was.

"Griff!"

Her voice came from his left.

He turned away from the voice and toward the source of the bullet, catching another flash of light. He vaulted up and toward the glint. His hand knocked the gun away as he slammed into the slight body in his path.

Jane Gross. It had to be. He wrapped an arm around her and pinned her to the floor.

Her harsh curses echoed in his ears.

The back door opened and a voice shouted, "Police!"

The lights flashed on. An officer stepped up to him and crouched down, brandishing handcuffs. "I've got her, sir."

Griff rolled off and let the officer cuff her. "The gun's over there somewhere," he said, picking himself up off the floor as police filled the room.

He whirled, apprehension squeezing his chest. "Sunny!"

Where was she? Was she all right?

SUNNY SAT UP, blinking in the bright light. She'd hit her head on the edge of the desk when she'd shoved the desk chair at Jane and dropped to the floor.

She had to get the book. Her head was fuzzy. She touched her temple and felt dampness.

Book? It took her a fraction of a second to remember.

Bess's book of children. She'd dropped it. She had to find it—it was her only bargaining chip. She felt around her until her fingers touched the smooth-grained leather.

A familiar voice echoed in her ears. She was still a little dazed. Had she dreamed Griff had saved her?

She slid the book into her pocket. She had to hold on to it.

"Sunny?"

There was his voice again. She blinked and cringed as a shadow towered over her.

Then strong familiar arms lifted her.

Griff.

"Are you hurt? Sunny? What happened to your head?"

She couldn't talk. All she could do was wrap her arms around him and burrow her nose in his neck. Eventually she realized she was crying, and he was holding her tightly.

"Have you been shot?" he asked. "Are you all right?"

His voice sounded strange—strained, unsteady.

All she could do was nod and cling to him. He was here. He'd found her.

Then Jane's harsh curses penetrated her confused brain and everything came back to her with brilliant clarity.

"Oh, my God! Emily!" She pushed at Griff's chest as panic filled her. "Where is she? Where's Mia?"

"It's okay." Griff kept one arm loosely around her and touched her face with his other hand. "The police have her. She's fine. We'll go see her in just a minute, after the EMTs make sure you're all right."

"No!" She shoved at him. "Now!" She broke away from him and pushed through the melee toward the door.

One of the officers grasped her arm, and she tried to shake free.

"No! Let me go!"

A female voice said, "Ma'am, I'll take you. They're just over here."

Still frantic, Sunny let the woman lead her out of the house. She searched the backyard, but didn't see anything except police cars.

The policewoman spoke on her shoulder mic, then pointed toward one of the police cars.

Sunny watched the passenger door open. Mia got out, holding Emily. Her precious baby.

With a cry of joy, Sunny ran, her arms out.

She grabbed up her daughter, her chest burning with relief. Her sweet, warm, soft baby. Happy cleansing tears streamed down her face.

"Oh, Emily…" she sobbed, hugging the tiny, familiar body against her, cradling the fine little head, hearing her frightened whimpers. "I was so afraid…"

Her heart felt like a big balloon, swelling with love.

"I know, baby," she murmured, trying to swallow her tears. She rocked Emily gently from side to side. "Mommy's scaring you. I'm so sorry, Emily. I'm so sorry. Mommy's got you now, and I will never ever let you go." She pressed her lips to one perfect little ear. "Mommy's got you now," she whispered on a quiet sob.

GRIFF TURNED AWAY. Blinking against the stinging in his eyes, he headed back toward the house. There was a lot of work to do before he was through here. For now, it was still his job.

That wasn't the only reason he'd turned away,

though. If he'd watched Sunny and her baby for another second, he'd have cried.

And Griffin Stone had never cried.

He'd seen his share of reunions. But none had ever affected him like this. The joy and love that radiated across Sunny's beautiful face as she held her baby penetrated him to the core.

His own heart swelled in echoed joy. He had kept his promise. He had helped her find her daughter. It was all she'd asked of him.

He ran his palm across his eyes as Captain Sparks approached.

"Good job, son."

"Thank you, Captain."

"And thank God there were no casualties."

Griff nodded.

"I have some news for you."

Griff sniffed and looked up.

"My dispatcher just called. A Hiram Cogburn showed up at the police station, declaring he has evidence that will put Jane and Ed Gross in prison for the rest of their lives. Says he followed you and Ms. Loveless here to Philadelphia."

"Cogburn?" Natasha had mentioned that name as the lawyer who drew up papers for Mia Raymond's adoption. "Does he have an old green Plymouth?"

"Should I ask?"

"Never mind. I'll check him out later."

Sparks shrugged. "I've got an officer taking his statement. Meanwhile, the officers here will sift through everything, looking for Ms. Raymond's book. I suppose you want to be in on the questioning of Jane Gross."

"Yes, sir, I do."

"We'll be talking to Mia Raymond, too."

Griff glanced back toward the car. "Take her to see her mother first."

SUNNY SAT IN THE BACKSEAT of the police car, with Emily's sweet head resting on her shoulder as she listened to her daughter's soft even breaths.

Her eyes burned from crying, and she couldn't stop smiling or kissing her sweet baby's face. Her heart ached with joy and relief. Every so often, a tear would escape and run down her cheek.

Beside her, Mia sat up. "They're arresting Aunt Janie."

Sunny opened her eyes. Two police officers were leading Jane Gross out of the house. But it wasn't Jane who held Sunny's attention.

Griff stood by the back door, talking with the police captain. He looked tired. His shoulders were not quite so square, and he occasionally rubbed his chest or wiped his face. His hair was tousled, as if he'd run his fingers through it countless times.

He glanced toward them. Sunny's heart fluttered. She couldn't see his eyes from here, but she felt them.

She'd gotten used to him being there. She'd allowed herself to believe in his promise of strength and safety. She'd fallen in love with him.

How was she going to live without him?

He and the captain turned and went back inside the house.

"Officer," Sunny said to the uniformed policewoman sitting in the driver's seat. "How much longer will they be in there?"

"I believe they're searching for a book, ma'am. Some sort of journal."

Mia gasped quietly. Emily cooed in her sleep.

The leather journal in Sunny's pocket. She'd forgotten all about it. She needed to give it to Griff. But first…

She glanced toward Mia, taking in her dark hair and wide eyes, the fine structure of her face and her slender grace. The niggling thought that had bothered her from the first moment she'd laid eyes on Mia began to fit together with other facts in her mind like pieces of a puzzle. Mia's age, her general appearance, the date Bess Raymond had written in her book.

If Sunny was right…a thrill swirled through her. "Is Jane really your aunt, Mia?"

"No."

"How is she connected with your mother?"

Mia let out a shaky breath. "Mom kept children for Jane for years. I think—" Her voice broke and she stopped.

Sunny shifted in her seat and looked at the teenager sitting beside her. "It's okay, Mia. We already know what Jane was doing."

"I…think she stole babies. I hadn't seen her in years. But when I was a kid, she came around all the time, always with a different baby."

A lump grew in Sunny's throat. "Do you know why your mother helped her?"

Mia put her fingers to her lips, stifling a little hiccupping sob. She hung her head and nodded. "Because of me."

Sunny's heart drummed against her chest wall. The erratic rhythm disturbed Emily and she began to whimper.

"Will you hold Emily for me?"

Mia looked up in surprise. "Sure."

Sunny kissed her baby and nuzzled her downy head. "Here's Mia, sweetie. You know Mia. She's been taking care of you."

With one hand still patting her baby as Mia held her, Sunny dug into her slacks pocket as her mind raced.

It all made sense—the date the Grosses had

disappeared from Nashville, the newspaper archive reporting a toddler missing from Centennial Park on the same day.

With fingers that shook, Sunny set the leather book on her knees.

"That's Mom's book."

She nodded. "Yes, it is. Officer, could you turn on the overhead light?"

The light flared.

On the very first page was the information Sunny sought. There, printed neatly, was the proof of Mia's identity.

Baby girl, eighteen months old, June 30, 1991, Nashville, Tennessee.

Sunny's heart skipped a beat. "Your mom isn't your real mother, is she?"

"Mom said the first moment she saw me she knew I was her daughter. My mom's a good person."

Sunny nodded. "I know she is."

"Mom kept me, and because of that, Janie made her keep the babies all those years." Mia took a sobbing breath. "I'm so sorry. I tried to take care of Emily. I'm so—"

"Mia." Sunny put her trembling hand on the girl's knee. "How did you get the name Mia?"

"Mom said it was what I called myself. She said it was more like Me-ann, but she named me Mia."

Sunny's heart pounded. Me-ann. Marianne. Everything made sense. But she had to be sure. She didn't want to hurt either Mia or Griff needlessly. "Look at me, Mia."

Mia raised her gaze to Sunny's. Her wide, dark-fringed eyes glittered in the harsh glow of the car's dome light.

Glittered like amethysts.

"Your eyes—"

Mia smiled sheepishly. "I know. They're weird. Mom says they're angels' eyes. Who ever heard of purple eyes?"

Laughter bubbled up from Sunny's chest. Joyous, healing laughter. "Oh, Mia. Your mom's right. They are angels' eyes. And I've heard of them. I've even seen them." She leaned over and hugged Mia, who looked at her quizzically.

A metallic voice sounded. The officer listened, then spoke.

"Yes, sir. On our way." She cranked the car.

Sunny started. "No, wait, what are you doing?"

"I've got orders to take both of you to the hospital."

"No! I have to talk to Griff—to Agent Stone."

"Sorry, ma'am. I was told to tell you that Special Agent Stone will meet you there later."

"But this is important."

"Yes, ma'am." The officer pulled out into the street and drove them away from Bess Raymond's house.

It wasn't until they reached the hospital that Sunny remembered she was holding the piece of evidence the police were after.

A DULL HEADACHE was hammering inside Griff's skull by the time he got to the hospital. The call had come through about a half hour ago.

Sunny had Bess's journal. She'd turned it over to the police officer who had driven them back to town. The officer had called Captain Sparks, and Sparks had told Griff.

They called off the search of Bess's house.

Jane's interrogation had to wait until morning, because she'd immediately demanded a lawyer. Griff needed to take a look at Bess's journal, and he still had to file his report. But first, he wanted to make sure Sunny was all right.

He pushed open the door into the intensive care waiting room, where he'd been told Sunny was waiting with Mia.

Sunny had her back to the door and was holding Emily. Bess's daughter, Mia, was sitting next to her, letting the baby grab at her finger. Both of them were laughing softly.

A shard of pain dulled by happiness for Sunny lodged in Griff's heart. He couldn't help but smile at her melodic laughter.

Dear God, he was going to miss her.

As the door swung shut behind him, Sunny turned her head. Her emerald-green eyes lit up when she saw him. She bent and kissed Emily's face and handed her over to Mia.

Then she rose and turned toward Griff.

He smiled at her and gave a little nod as his throat clogged with emotion. This was what he had promised her. And no rescue, no triumph, no solved case had ever come close to how he felt now, knowing she and her baby were safe and reunited.

Sunny's face lit in a tremulous smile and she flew into his arms, startling him with her ferocity.

He pulled her tightly to him, cradling the back of her head and pressing his nose into her hair.

"Oh, Griff, how can I ever—"

"Shh. You did it. You found Emily. You got your happy ending."

He felt a sob shudder through her.

"Is everything okay? How's she doing?"

Sunny pulled back enough to look into his eyes, and the sheer happiness that surrounded her like a bright glow sent his heart soaring.

Then before his eyes, she became somber.

"Sunny, what's the matter? Isn't Emily all right?"

Sunny nodded. "She's wonderful. And she's dying to meet her valiant rescuer."

Then she put her palm against his cheek. "But there's someone else you need to meet first." Her voice quavered, but her eyes glittered with anticipation.

Griff frowned. "Yeah? Who?" Why was she acting so strangely?

Sunny stepped out of the circle of his arms and turned toward Mia. Griff followed her gaze.

The teenager had secured Emily in her infant carrier and was cooing at her.

"Mia. Come here. There's someone I want you to meet."

Mia looked up, then picked up the carrier and stepped around the couch.

Sunny took Emily.

Griff watched them with an odd sense of apprehension. He rubbed the aching spot in the middle of his chest as he looked at Bess's daughter.

"Griff?" Sunny's voice was choked.

He glanced at her and saw tears filling her eyes. She smiled.

"Sunny, what is it—?" The burning in his chest increased.

He looked back at Mia. She had the careless

beauty of a teenager. Flawless skin, dark, shiny hair, but she also was oddly familiar. High cheekbones, wide mouth, large, dark-lashed eyes. Then he met her gaze.

Shock ripped through him. He almost staggered under the impact.

His first thought—*damn*. His first thought was ridiculous. What the hell was wrong with him?

He tore his gaze away from the violet eyes staring back at him and looked questioningly, fearfully, at Sunny. "What's going on?" He heard the note of panic that was fast stealing his breath.

Sunny's tear-streaked face beamed like an angel. "Griff. Mia is Marianne. Your sister."

"No!" Stunned, he held up his hands to ward off the cruel joke. He squeezed his eyes shut. "What the hell are you saying?"

"Griff. It's true. Believe me."

Sunny's lilting voice floated around him. He wanted to swing his fists at it. To stop it.

He steeled himself, then met Mia's gaze again. She was still looking at him as if he were some insanely famous rock star or something. Her jewel-like gaze never wavered.

Suddenly, he couldn't see. His own eyes were full of tears.

He'd never cried, not even when he'd lost her. Not when he'd thought he'd failed Sunny. Never.

He put out a shaking hand and Mia stepped toward him. Her face was wet with tears, her outstretched fingers trembling.

Their fingers touched, and Griff's breath caught in a sob. He pulled her to him. She wrapped her arms around his waist and hugged him tightly.

And he cried.

SUNNY WAITED NERVOUSLY for Griff in their hotel room. He'd called about ten minutes before to ask if it was okay if he came by to shower and change.

Mia had insisted on staying at the hospital with her mother, and Griff had stayed with her.

In her carrier, Emily emitted a quiet sigh. She'd had a long day. Sunny had held her until she squirmed and whined. Then she'd reluctantly put her in her carrier, where Emily had immediately gone to sleep.

Now Sunny paced. She'd tried to lie down, but she hadn't even been able to close her eyes. She was too keyed up.

She was worried about Griff. She'd watched him when he'd realized Mia truly was his sister. He'd turned pale as a ghost. His eyes had streamed tears, and his face had nearly crumpled.

Nearly.

Something was wrong and she knew it. He'd

been quiet and withdrawn afterward, as he and Mia talked.

Feeling as if she was intruding, Sunny had insisted on taking a taxi from the hospital to the hotel. Once she'd closed the door to her room, she'd hugged Emily and wept, spilling out all the tension of the past six days, until she'd ended up too tired to cry any longer.

She heard the unmistakable sound of a plastic key card tripping an electronic lock. Griff was here.

She stopped pacing and stared at the door as it opened slowly.

His hair was still a mess. His face under a day's worth of stubble was drawn and pale. His eyes shone darkly. He closed the door, and slowly raised his head. But he never quite met her gaze. His face appeared haunted.

"Griff? Are you okay?"

He didn't answer. He shrugged out of the wrinkled sport coat he'd worn all day, and began to unbutton his shirt, heading for the bathroom.

"Griff?"

"I'm going to shower now." His voice was hoarse. He closed the door to the bathroom and she heard the shower come on.

Behind her, she heard Emily whimper, then start to cry. Sunny hurried over to the infant carrier and picked up her baby. "Hi, sweetie. I didn't mean to wake you." She bounced her gently in her arms. "It's been a long day, hasn't it?" She touched her lips to Emily's downy head and breathed deeply of her sweet, baby-powder scent.

In almost no time, Griff came out of the bathroom dressed in his jeans with his shirt open. His chest and abdomen glistened with dampness, and his hair was spiked where he'd toweled it dry. His eyes were rimmed with red as his gaze roamed over her and lingered on Emily. His brows drew down.

"Thanks."

"This is your room."

Emily whimpered.

"How is she?"

Sunny smiled. "She's fine. Griff, I never got a chance to thank you."

He stepped closer and peered down at the baby. He touched her tiny hand with one finger, and gently ran his thumb along her downy hairline. His shoulders bowed and he hung his head.

A drop of water, or a tear, splashed on Sunny's forearm.

"Griff, what's the matter?" Sunny asked, apprehension clogging the back of her throat. He was acting so odd.

He didn't answer.

"How—how did it go with Mia?"

He shook his head. "Mia. Marianne. My sis—" He stopped and cleared his throat. "I'd given up hope."

"No, you hadn't. I didn't know what you were searching for, but your belief gave me the hope to go on."

"You've been remarkably strong through all of this," he said gruffly.

"No, it was you—"

"You know I never believed in your happy endings. I've seen a lot of happiness and a lot of heartache in my work. You must have gotten a kick out of discovering that Mia is my sister."

Sunny shook her head, but before she could say anything else, Griff continued, still looking down at Emily.

"When she was Emily's age, I changed her diapers. I taught her to say her name. She couldn't say it quite right. It always came out Me-ann. I guess that's where Mia came from."

"What's she going to do now?"

He sighed and glanced up briefly. "Bess Raymond's testimony will bring closure to a lot of people. I doubt, with her age and illness, that she'll have to do any time." He smiled sadly. "Mia is her daughter. That's not going to change."

"But you'll see her. You'll get to know her, let her get to know you."

He nodded, his eyes bright with tears. Then he blinked and looked back at Emily. He held out his finger and Emily grabbed it. He made a small, anguished sound and gently pulled away. When he met her gaze again, his unleashed pain streaked through her.

"This isn't about Mia, is it?" Sunny's throat closed up. She tried to swallow. "What's the matter?"

Sighing, he ran a palm over his clean-shaven face and took a step away from her. "I tried so hard not to love you."

Love you. She blinked. Had she heard right? Pain stabbed her in the middle of her chest.

He shook his head. "I always managed to stay away from the families' deepest sadness and their greatest joys. I thought if I ever let myself feel all that, I'd—" he swallowed, then shrugged and lowered his gaze "—I'd fall into some kind of bottomless pit and be lost forever. Lord knows hovering on the edge of it was bad enough."

Sunny couldn't stop the smile that softened her lips. She'd have sworn her heart couldn't swell any more, it was so full of love and relief and happiness. But apparently the heart's capacity for love was infinite, because she loved Griff.

"Now you have your happy ending," she whispered. "And you didn't fall into the pit."

"Not yet." He looked away and wiped his eyes. "I never met anyone who compares with you. You found my heart. I didn't even know it was still—" He stopped. His jaw flexed.

He sniffed and blinked. Then he held out his hand.

She took a step toward him and waited.

His face began to relax, and his beautiful violet eyes never wavered.

Finally his mouth turned up in a little smile. "I love you—" His voice broke.

Sunny shifted Emily to her other side and stepped into the circle of Griff's arms. "I love you, too," she whispered. "I think I've loved you a long time."

Griff's lips were against her ear. "I know what you mean."

Then he ran his lips across her cheek and kissed her. Sunny's insides turned to hot flowing lava as their kiss deepened and heated.

He pulled her against him, holding her in the circle of his safe, strong, sexy body, with Emily tucked between them. The baby waved her arms and Griff let her grab his finger.

"Now," he whispered against her lips. "If you'll marry me, we can have our very own happy ending."

"Oh, Griff." Sunny laughed. Then she thought about what marriage would mean.

"Will we have to move to Washington, D.C.?"

Griff watched the baby, his eyes dark and soft. "No. I turned in my resignation before I left, remember? Decker knows I'm quitting."

"You're going to stay in Nashville?"

"I grew up there. And it's where you are." He kissed her cheek, then nipped at her ear, sending shivers through her.

"But what are you going to do?"

"I was kind of hoping Loveless, Inc. might have an opening."

"For a 'happy endings' detective?"

He bent and kissed Emily's tiny fingers. "You take the happy endings cases. I'll be the hard-boiled private eye."

"So…Loveless and Stone?"

"Stone and Loveless." He kissed her gently.

"We'll negotiate," she whispered against his lips.

"Now this is a happy ending."

Emily giggled.

Sunny shook her head. "Not a happy ending, a happy beginning."

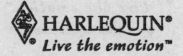

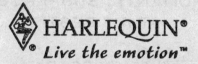

Harlequin Historicals®
Historical Romantic Adventure!

From rugged lawmen and valiant knights to defiant heiresses and spirited frontierswomen, Harlequin Historicals will capture your imagination with their dramatic scope, passion and adventure.

Harlequin Historicals...
they're too good to miss!

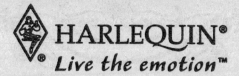
HARLEQUIN®
Live the emotion™

Upbeat,
All-American Romances

flipside

Romantic Comedy

Harlequin Historicals®

Historical,
Romantic Adventure

HARLEQUIN®
INTRIGUE

Romantic Suspense

HARLEQUIN®
HARLEQUIN ROMANCE®

The essence of
modern romance

HARLEQUIN®
Presents

Seduction and passion
guaranteed

HARLEQUIN *Super*ROMANCE®

Emotional,
Exciting, Unexpected

Temptation

Sassy, Sexy, Seductive!

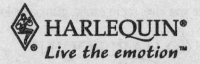

HARLEQUIN®
Presents

The world's bestselling romance series...
The series that brings you your favorite authors,
month after month:

Helen Bianchin...Emma Darcy
Lynne Graham...Penny Jordan
Miranda Lee...Sandra Marton
Anne Mather...Carole Mortimer
Susan Napier...Michelle Reid

and many more uniquely talented authors!

Wealthy, powerful, gorgeous men...
Women who have feelings just like your own...
The stories you love, set in exotic, glamorous locations...

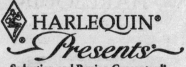

Seduction and Passion Guaranteed!

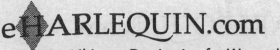